E*Wally
and
the
Quest

D0377765

E-Wally and the Quest: Book One in The Adventures of E-Wally
by Judy Shasek and Wendy Anderson Schulz

Published by Net Works Publishing, Inc. For more information, visit: www.e-wally.org

Cover Illustration by Jonathan Wilson. For more info, visit www.jwstudio.com

Cover and Interior Design & Layout by Pneuma Books: Complete Publisher's Services
For more info, visit www.pneumadesign.com/books/info.htm
Titling set in Font in a Red Suit 72pt. Body set in Journal Text 11.75/16 pt.

FIRST PRINTING
Printing in the United States of America by Thomson-Shore
08 07 06 05 04 03 02 01   08 07 06 05 04 03 02 01

Publisher's Cataloging-in-Publication Data
(Provided by Quality Books, Inc)

Shasek, Judy.
        E-Wally and the quest / by Judy Shasek and Wendy Anderson Schulz. -- 1st ed.
        p.cm. -- (The adventures of E-Wally)
        SUMMARY: When Justin meets E-Wally, the e-boy who delivers his e-mail,
he finds that his technological educatio is just beginning.
        LCCN 2001091804
        ISBN 0-9711818-0-2

        1. Computers--Juvenile fiction. 2. Education--Juvenile fiction. 3. Technology--
Juvenile fiction. [1. Computers--Fiction. 2. Education--Fiction. 3. Technology--
Fiction.] I. Schulz, Wendy Anderson. II. Title.

        PZ7.S532395Ew 2001   [Fic]
                                QBI01-700815

E*Wally and the Quest

THE ADVENTURES OF E*WALLY

by Judy Shasek & Wendy Anderson Schulz
Illustration by Jonathan Wilson

Published by
Net Works Publishing

To Pete, my friend, my hero, my husband,
thank you for supporting my quest. I love you.
—WS

✳

To Eddie, who always supports the meanderings
of my enthusiasm and energies, my best friend.
To Ed and Kristy who consistently feed my
spirit and imagination
—JS

✳

To children and their parents who grow closer
through sharing the adventure of learning together.

TABLE OF CONTENTS

THE ADVENTURE CONTINUES AT

WWW.E-WALLY.ORG

★ Explore E-Wally's on-line activities

★ Build your own games and websites

★ Learn how to stay safe on-line

★ Bring E-Wally to school. All on-line
  activities have an easy to follow lesson
  plan for classroom use.

```
01000010 01100101 01110111 01100001 01110010 01100101 00100000
01101111 01100110 00100000 01110100 01101000 01100101 00100000
01000111 01101100 01101111 01100010 01100001 01101100 00100000
01001000 01100001 01100011 01101011 01100101 01110010 00100000
01000111 01100001 01101110 01100111 00101110 00101110 00101110
01000010 01100101 01110111 01100001 01110010 01100101 00100000
01101111 01100110 00100000 01110100 01101000 01100101 00100000
01000111 01101100 01101111 01100010 01100001 01101100 00100000
01001000 01100001 01100011 01101011 01100101 01110010 00100000
01000111 01100001 01101110 01100111 00101110 00101110 00101110
01000010 01100101 01110111 01100001 01110010 01100101 00100000
01101111 01100110 00100000 01110100 01101000 01100101 00100000
01000111 01101100 01101111 01100010 01100001 01101100 00100000
01001000 01100001 01100011 01101011 01100101 01110010 00100000
01000111 01100001 01101110 01100111 00101110 00101110 00101110
01000010 01100101 01110111 01100001 01110010 01100101 00100000
01101111 01100110 00100000 01110100 01101000 01100101 00100000
01000111 01101100 01101111 01100010 01100001 01101100 00100000
01001000 01100001 01100011 01101011 01100101 01110010 00100000
01000111 01100001 01101110 01100111 00101110 00101110 00101110
01000010 01100101 01110111 01100001 01110010 01100101 00100000
01101111 01100110 00100000 01110100 01101000 01100101 00100000
01000111 01101100 01101111 01100010 01100001 01101100 00100000
01001000 01100001 01100011 01101011 01100101 01110010 00100000
01000111 01100001 01101110 01100111 00101110 00101110 00101110
01000010 01100101 01110111 01100001 01110010 01100101 00100000
01101111 01100110 00100000 01110100 01101000 01100101 00100000
01000111 01101100 01101111 01100010 01100001 01101100 00100000
01001000 01100001 01100011 01101011 01100101 01110010 00100000
01000111 01100001 01101110 01100111 00101110 00101110 00101110
01000010 01100101 01110111 01100001 01110010 01100101 00100000
01101111 01100110 00100000 01110100 01101000 01100101 00100000
01000111 01101100 01101111 01100010 01100001 01101100 00100000
01001000 01100001 01100011 01101011 01100101 01110010 00100000
01000111 01100001 01101110 01100111 00101110 00101110 00101110
01000010 01100101 01110111 01100001 01110010 01100101 00100000
01101111 01100110 00100000 01110100 01101000 01100101 00100000
```

A MENACING MESSAGE

A loud boom broke the morning silence as someone pounded on the gray metallic door. The door of E-Wally's house shuddered, as a crumpled and dirty scrap of paper was glued to its center by a fist covered in gross-smelling slime. Startled by both the disgusting smell and the ominous sound, E-Wally's head jerked up from where he had been stuffing packets into his mailbag. There was only one person who emitted a smell so caustic and terrible — Olla Brac. She never visited any home in the Land of the Internet unless there was trouble, big trouble, for a poor e-person living there. E-Wally's stomach churned with fear. "Grandpa!"

E-Wally was the oldest son in a hard-working family of e-people. Deep in the Land of the Internet, e-people had the job of delivering humans' e-mail and website packets. Pushing aside his mailbag and leaping to his feet, E-Wally raced to the other side of his house and barged, panting, into the kitchen. Grandpa and Mom sat at the small brushed-metal table. "Honey," said Mom reaching out with a jam covered bread-byte, not noticing the look of pure fear on her ten-year-old son's face, "have some breakfast before work."

"Mom, Grandpa, don't you smell it? It's her. She stuck something on our door." Looking worriedly toward his very rickety and old Grandpa, E-Wally said, "Stay there. I'll see if she's gone." Before his grandpa, E-Liam, could rise from his bulky metal chair E-Wally darted out of the kitchen.

E-Wally crept to the living room window and lifted his eyes cautiously over the sill. Looking out, E-Wally saw a dark swarm of bugs following a grotesque figure as it plodded away toward the flickering wires of the Internet. E-Wally silently pulled open the front door and gasped at the sight and smell of the message on the door. In blood red letters was scrawled the name "E-Liam." E-Wally solemnly pulled the paper from the sticky glop that had come from Olla's reeking hands. Holding his nose with one hand, he carried the foul note to his grandpa.

"Is she gone?" asked Grandpa seriously, reaching for the note and choking back a retch at the smell of the putrid paper.

E-Wally nodded, glancing apprehensively at his mom whose face was ashen.

Grandpa opened the note, held it at arm's length to keep the smell as far away as possible, then read aloud, "Take heed at my warning, e-sir. Your wretched age and weak body do not excuse you from doing your share of deliveries. There is no room for the old and slow in the Land of the Internet. You will do double deliveries for one week. If you fail to complete all tasks then prepare for your punishment. Our null bin has not had any action in quite some time."

The e-family sat pale and silent at their kitchen table. The silence was broken suddenly by E-Wally's urgent plea, "Grandpa, we've got to do something. You can't carry the overload of packets you already have, forget about a double assignment. Maxter and I will help you, but it is still impossible. She's trying to kill you with work. That miserable hag would be happy to send you to the null bin. She wants that."

The null bin was death. No one had ever returned from the null bin and rumor had it that e-people sent there were vaporized along with their packets. Grandpa was the hardest working and most respected member of the e-community. He knew that no one ignored an order from Olla Brac. Her power over the e-people was unquestionable. "E-Wally, I will do what she asks. It's my only chance."

"Forget it Grandpa," raged E-Wally. "You can barely move when you come home from work. Your back is broken every night. Look at your face — you're pale and sick. No, no, that horrible, bug-infested witch isn't going to take you Grandpa. We need to do something. We can all fight her off."

"Stop," shrieked Mom in horror. No one disrespected the orders of either Olla Brac or her master, the evil King Henry. "E-Wally, her bugs could be in this kitchen right now. She could be hearing every word we say. You can't fight it. We will manage. We'll all pull together and help Grandpa through this."

"Do you think she'll stop at that?" retorted E-Wally, desperate to make his family listen. "She'll keep threatening us as long as King Henry has us in his control. We have to do something. There has to be a way to get rid of her. Grandpa, please. We have to fight this."

Grandpa turned hard but loving eyes on his usually cheerful and obedient grandson. "No. E-Wally, there'll not be another word about fighting. Olla Brac and King Henry are in control. That is just the way things are. We'll manage together." Grandpa paused, then reached out a hand to touch E-Wally on the shoulder.

Like an explosion, E-Wally erupted from the table. The heavy metal of his chair shrieked loudly across the kitchen floor. "If you won't do anything, fine. I'll do it myself!"

Frustrated and furious, he flew out the kitchen door. He grabbed his overstuffed mailbag, strode through the living room, and grabbed a dozen of Grandpa's packets. He tucked them under his arm and stomped out the door. Overloaded with packets, E-Wally jumped heavily onto his bulky, dented transport board and set off to work.

✦

That evening, in another home, in another world, things were no more peaceful. Eleven-year-old Justin bolted from the dinner table with his mother's words trailing behind him in an angry stream.

"I'm serious Justin — no e-mail and no surfing the Web! You have to work on that dinosaur worksheet all night. That's it! Nothing else!" Justin's Mom grabbed his backpack from the kitchen corner where it had been all afternoon. "Here, you might just need these, don't you think?" added Mom with a frown, giving Justin one of those looks that moms do so well.

Grabbing the backpack, Justin stomped up the stairs toward his room.

"I hate dinosaurs," shouted Justin slamming his door shut. "Why do I need to know about dinosaurs anyway? They're dead, that's all I need to know," he grumbled to himself.

It was already Monday night and the long twenty-five question worksheet was due first thing on Wednesday morning. In one frustrated motion, Justin threw his books onto his bed and sat down at his computer. He logged onto the Internet to see if he had any new e-mail.

Meanwhile, the Land of the Internet was buzzing, humming, and digitally zipping along deep in the telephone lines and wires across the planet. E-Wally had just finished delivering all of his own assignments plus a dozen of his grandpa's. He was exhausted. Olla's warning had pushed E-Wally to the limit. He wasn't thinking straight; he wasn't even thinking. At the very moment Justin logged onto his e-mail, E-Wally broke the cardinal rule of his land. Bumping along on his slow, ancient surfboard with his blond buzz-cut hair standing on end, E-Wally was heading toward a server. As an e-person, he had one job: deliver humans' e-mail packets to the server, then make a hasty return to get another delivery. The first rule, the most important rule, in the Land of the Internet was that no e-person would ever go past the server.

But that rule would not be obeyed by this e-boy tonight. E-Wally was angry, frustrated, and desperate to find a way to help his grandpa. Without thinking of the consequences, he decided to jump on the POP3 line and go all the way through this server and to a human's modem. Once he got to the modem he would hide out and devise a plan.

At that same moment, Justin's dark brown eyes quickly scanned his e-mail list. A new e-mail had just arrived from his best friend, Steve. With a quick click Justin selected the message. When Justin opened the message, he noticed something strange about this e-mail. He leaned forward, pushing his face close to the screen. "What?" Justin wondered, brushing a shiny lock of brown hair from his eyes so he could see better. The letters in Steve's name were all smushed and the S was lying on its side. "What happened?" Justin said to himself. "I've never seen anything like that."

Justin took his mouse and dragged it to where *Steve* was written. Just then the craziest thing happened. Like a line of dominoes, the letters began to fall down. Justin could see something moving across the letters. He stopped moving his mouse and leaned into the screen. He looked so close that his freckled nose touched the screen. Something was moving, but all Justin could see was a small blob.

Justin raced to his bed, knelt on the floor, and pulled out a large box of junk. Tossing a flattened football, an old candy wrapper, and six toy soldiers aside, he grabbed what he had been looking for – a large silver magnifying glass. He kicked the box back under his bed and dashed back to the monitor. With his magnifying glass Justin examined the small blob on the screen.

"Wow!" yelled Justin as he jumped back from his computer. The blob wasn't a blob – it was a boy! Justin gaped at the image a second time. How could a boy be in his computer? When Justin peered through his magnifying glass again, he saw it more clearly. There was indeed a tiny, blond-haired boy hiding behind the letter b! The boy was trembling and scared, trying not to be seen.

"Who are you?" asked Justin.

The boy did not respond.

"Who are you?" Justin questioned a second time, this time a little louder. Again the boy did not respond. *Maybe he can't hear me in there*, Justin thought to himself. "Who are you?" Justin yelled as he peered through the magnifying glass.

To the tiny boy in the computer the magnifying glass had made Justin's eye look fifty feet wide. E-Wally froze at the sight of his first human! He had no time to think, for at that moment the giant eye came even closer. Horrified, he jumped out from behind the b and ran, tripping over an r an o and a t before taking cover behind an h.

Hearing her older brother yelling, Justin's always-curious little sister, Ruthie, snuck to the partially open bedroom door and peered in. It was a curious scene. Ruthie silently pushed the door open a bit more, slid quietly along the wall, and noiselessly scrambled under the bed. Ruthie strained her neck out past the foot of the bed. *He's weirder than I thought*, she mused to herself. Although Ruthie, at nine, was two years younger than Justin, she thought herself to be much smarter and a whole lot more clever than her intense older brother.

Maybe I scared him, Justin thought. *Maybe he can't hear me*. He needed a different approach. Biting his lower lip Justin tried to figure out what to do. Suddenly, he had an idea. Starting at the bottom of his message from Steve, which was now not much of a message since half of the letters were knocked over and the other half were smushed, Justin started to delete the letters. Justin worked slowly, keeping the cursor far from the tiny boy in the computer. When all of the letters were erased, except for the *h* the boy was hiding behind, Justin started to type. "Who are you?" Justin waited to see what would happen.

There was no response from the scared boy hiding behind the *h*. It was hard for Justin to hold the magnifying glass and type at the same time so he adjusted the zoom on his computer screen to two hundred percent. Now he could easily see the boy. With the magnifying glass gone, E-Wally could see that what had looked like a giant monster's eye was just the deep brown eye of a boy like himself. The boy was big, but he was no cycloptic monster.

Justin typed one more time, "Who are you?"

E-Wally slowly came out from behind the *h* and walked over to where Justin had typed. All of a sudden more letters popped up on Justin's screen. "E - W - A - L - L - Y."

"E-Wally," Justin said. "Your name is E-Wally?" Justin typed back. Once again letters popped up on Justin's screen.

"Yes," E-Wally replied halfway regretting his hasty decision to sneak into a modem. Still he was very curious. There was no question that he was somehow communicating with his very first human. More words popped up on Justin's screen. "Where am I?" E-Wally asked, taking his eye off the large human long enough to scan the vast gray emptiness with its huge wall of letters separating E-Wally from some other colorful world.

Justin answered, eagerly typing as fast as he could: "My name is Justin. This is so random. You're in my monitor. How'd you get in there? What are you? Who are you?"

E-Wally sat down on the letter *J* and sent back an answer, "I am an e-boy. I deliver your e-mail. Actually I am not an e-deliverer anymore, I ran away."

Justin prodded skeptically, "An e-deliverer? Is this some kind of joke?"

"Just look at me, of course I'm an e-boy!" E-Wally declared pulling at his shirt and pointing to his cap.

Justin scratched his head. An e-mailman? He did look like a mailman. E-Wally wore a pair of long blue pants with a thin yellow line down the side. His matching blue shirt had a small yellow emblem that looked like an envelope. Under the envelope the name E-*Wally* was printed neatly. E-Wally's hat was actually more like a cap; it looked like the kind of cap that Justin had seen milkmen wear in old movies. It sat on the back of E-Wally's head allowing the spikes of E-Wally's buzz cut to poke out every which way.

"You deliver my e-mails? Wow, I never thought much about how e-mail gets delivered. I thought they just shot on over to other computers," typed a surprised Justin.

"That's silly. Of course someone has to deliver them. There are millions of us in here, just like there are lots of you out there," continued E-Wally. He was still a bit wary of this human since he had been taught to be very careful while delivering packets, making sure to never be seen by the humans. Legends were told of e-people who'd been seen by humans. They were never heard from again. But the human boy was smiling, he seemed friendly enough and there was a wall of glass separating them.

Then Justin asked, "Where's your family?" As he waited for E-Wally's reply, Justin tucked his long legs under him, balancing on the two yellow bean-bags he used for a desk chair.

E-Wally eagerly told Justin all about his people, the e-people. "My grandfather E-Liam is the greatest. We all live together — my mom, grandpa, me, and my lit-tle brother, Maxter." He told Justin how everyone in his family had delivered information packets, along with all the other E-people, for generations. E-Wally explained how they worked all day long racing from servers to routers, from routers through repeaters, from repeaters to servers, all the while carrying heavy packs full of bits and bytes. "You know," E-Wally ended his story with the one scary thought that wouldn't leave the back of his mind, "no e-person is ever, never, ever allowed to go past the server and into a modem. The rule of the Land of the Internet is that if a human spots an e-person they will delete us and we will go to the recycle bin, whatever that is." E-Wally shuddered for a second remembering Olla's threats about the null bin.

"No way. Like I'd really send you to the recycle bin. You must've been freaked out when you saw me. Why'd you come here? Why'd you run away?" Justin typed.

"A terrible ruler, King Henry, reigns over the Land of the Internet. King Henry makes us work without stopping. If we do anything wrong, he sets a foul woman named Olla Brac and her bugs after us. He makes us work faster and longer every day. My grandpa can't keep up. I've gotta find a way to help him. My brother, Maxter, is too little and my father and uncle are..." E-Wally paused, "well they aren't around. So there's only me. I've gotta find somewhere safe for him to go."

Justin thought of his own grandpa. It'd be terrible if Gramps never got to rest or had to carry heavy stuff all day. Gramps had a sore back and loved taking a nap after lunch. Justin thought hard. "I know, I'll hide you in my hard drive until we make a plan. You sure came to the right place."

"What's a hard drive?" asked E-Wally.

"It's a place I can store my files separate from every other computer in the world. Hold on E-Wally, I'll show you."

Justin saved the remains of the e-mail that E-Wally was standing in as a document onto his hard drive. Then he disconnected from the Internet and opened E-Wally's file. "You should be safe now."

E-Wally walked around the blank screen. The vast emptiness of the document was worlds different from the warmth of the humming Internet lines. E-Wally felt a knot tightening in the pit of his stomach and his hands grew clammy. The reality of running away began to sink in. As E-Wally looked around at his new surroundings, he could hear the sound of Justin typing him a new message. The sound of his new friend's typing calmed the wild butterflies thrashing around in poor E-Wally's stomach.

Justin took one look at his new friend's face and mistook nervousness for boredom. "I guess there isn't anything for you to do, huh?" Justin typed. "Wait, I have an idea, I'll download you a house from the Web."

Without waiting for E-Wally to answer him, Justin closed the file with E-Wally in it and logged back onto the Internet. Justin typed in a search for "houses." Then he had an even better idea, he deleted "houses" and typed in "tree houses." Justin discovered a web page with pictures of the coolest tree houses he had ever seen. He selected a perfect tree house, one that he would have loved to have in his own backyard. Justin copied the picture of the tree house and logged back off the Internet. He opened the document with E-Wally in it.

✳

CHAPTER TWO

A POWERFUL PROPHECY

While Justin was on the Internet searching for tree houses, E-Wally had typed, "NO! NO! NO! NO! NO! NO! NO! NO! NO! NO! NO! NO! NO WEB PAGES!"

Justin was shocked. "Wow, chill out E-Wally! What's wrong with web pages?"

"NO WEB PAGES! King Henry's decreed it – no e-people can *ever* go into a web page. It's forbidden." E-Wally ran behind the letter J and hung onto it, trembling.

Wow, thought Justin to himself, *my parents and*

teachers have lots of rules for me, but he's got tons more.
The Internet didn't seem that full of rules when Justin
was surfing websites and sending e-mail.

"Gosh, sorry, E-Wally. I just thought you would like
a tree house while you were hiding out in my hard
drive. I know I'd like to live in a tree house if I ran away
from home."

The two boys were quiet for a while. Justin was disappointed that E-Wally didn't want the tree house he'd
picked out. Then Justin had an idea. "E-Wally, you said
that King Henry decreed that you couldn't go into a
web page. Well, guess what. I don't want you to go
to one, I just downloaded part of it."

E-Wally slowly came out from the J. "I guess it might
be okay," E-Wally typed back.

A smile came to Justin's face and he bounced atop
his beanbags. He was so excited for his new friend to
play in the tree house. Justin cut and pasted the tree
house near E-Wally. E-Wally leaned against the J
and looked at the tree house. He had never seen anything like it. Slowly E-Wally walked closer and closer to the tree house. It was amazing, tucked into an
enormous banyan tree with wide leafy branches that
spread from just over E-Wally's head all the way to
the top of the document file.

E-Wally carefully climbed up the rope ladder and
explored his new hideout. The red canvas roof was
wider than the tree house and shaded the two side win-

dows from the enormous yellow sun that sparkled through the canopy of deep green leaves. In an instant he had scrambled up and climbed inside the tree house. "I've never seen anything like this, ever!" E-Wally exclaimed. He loved it, Justin just knew he would.

Since King Henry had taken over the land, the e-people had been forced into working and working without rest. Like all the other e-children, E-Wally had never had a vacation, or much time to play, run, or even just mess around with his best friends, Pete and Eddie. Now he had a tire swing, a slide, and a rope to climb on. E-Wally was nonstop action, trying out everything again and again.

Justin burst with pride. He had really created an incredible file for E-Wally. "You couldn't be happy staying in that boring blank document. Look at the leaves, the sky, the sun. Do you have all those colors in the Land of the Internet?"

E-Wally glanced overhead to the lush green leaves rustling overhead and at the bright red canopy roof atop the dark wooden tree house perched off the ground. "This is beautiful. My land is more electric-colored and metal. We have gold, orange, grays, and black mostly," explained E-Wally, sprinting over to the ladder. Justin watched E-Wally play in his tree house for a long time. The friends typed dozens of messages, chatting and laughing as easily as any other two boys playing together.

Under the bed, Ruthie was completely hypnotized by the sight of E-Wally scrambling all over the tree house. Startled by the sound of Mom's footsteps on the stairs, Ruthie quickly turned and clunked her head on the foot of Justin's bed. Muffling her "ouch!" with cupped hands, she hurriedly belly-crawled out from under the bed, to the door and into the hall. Ruthie hopped to her feet and bolted into her own room. She landed on her bed in one giant leap, making it just in time to miss her mother turning the corner toward the children's rooms. As Justin was typing another message to E-Wally, he heard a knock on his door.

"Justin! Lights out in five minutes kiddo! Have you finished your dinosaur worksheet?" his mom asked from the hallway outside the closed door.

He had been having so much fun with his new friend, he hadn't realized how late it was. Justin's face went white with fear. "Oh, sure Mom. I'm... I'm... I'm going to bed – goodnight!" Justin leaped up and quickly turned out the light so Mom would think he was sleeping. She couldn't find out he had not finished that worksheet. She'd be sure to ground him off the computer if he didn't get it done.

In the dark, Justin typed quietly as if in a whisper, "E-Wally, I have to go. Stay in your tree house. I'll see you tomorrow."

Grinning, E-Wally stuck his head out of the tree

house window. "Okay, Justin, no problem. I could stay here forever. Thanks for hiding me."

✦

As E-Wally was going to sleep for his very first night away from home, back at home his little curly haired brother, Maxter could not sleep at all. Six-year-old Maxter kneeled silently on his bed staring out his bedroom window. Where was E-Wally? Would he ever come back? It was long past his bedtime, but he was far from being sleepy. The sight of E-Wally's empty bed was too much for Maxter. Although he was too young to remember it, his Uncle Anzwar had disappeared, then his dad, and now E-Wally was gone, and Olla was threatening to take Grandpa. Maxter burst into tears at the thought of it all.

E-Liam raised his tired body from the kitchen table and headed upstairs. "I'll check on Maxter on my way to bed," he said to his daughter, giving her a comforting pat on the arm.

"Good night, Dad," she said staring at the front door praying it would burst open with E-Wally full of apologies for being so very late.

E-Liam could hear Maxter crying before he reached the little boy's room. He quietly entered the room and sat at the foot of Maxter's bed. Maxter turned to see who it was and quickly wiped his tear-soaked face. He dried his runny nose with the sleeve of his pajama top.

"Come on over here. You're such a big guy already. You and E-Wally have grown up too quickly right under my nose. It's no wonder you're confused and worried. There's so much about your history that you need to know. I should have taken the time to tell both of you boys."

"I'm big?" asked Maxter cheering up a bit.

"Absolutely," said Grandpa, smiling at Maxter as he settled in under his quilt. "If you're not too tired, I'll tell you the tale of our people."

"I'm not too tired."

"Okay then, let's start at the beginning. Way back in the 1970s life was slow. Before it was called the Land of the Internet, our land was called ARPAnet. Queen Cyberlina was the ruler of the land. She knew us all by name. Our land was like a small town. We'd wave to each other as we went on our way delivering packets to secret government projects, exciting scientific projects, and to the great thinkers of the day. Sometimes I'd bring a freshly baked bread-byte to the fuzzball router just outside Washington, D.C. He was a great guide, always helpful and always saving me lots of time. Why some days I was finished with my entire route before sunset."

"A guide? They aren't guides!" exclaimed Maxter, his eyes wide with surprise. "Fuzzball routers make us go slow. Why would you *ever* give him anything Grandma made?"

Grandpa pulled Maxter in close, "Because," he whispered, "before King Henry it was very, very different. Fuzzball routers were friendly, helpful guides."

Maxter was really confused now. "What happened to Queen Cyberlina? Why is King Henry in power? How did things get so bad?" And then he blurted out, "Where did E-Wally go? Is he coming back or is he going to be gone forever like Uncle Anzwar and Dad?"

"One thing at a time. I know this is tough Maxter, but I can't bring back Uncle Anzwar or your dad. All we can do is keep our hope strong that wherever they are they are safe and will come back one day. For now, we need to be strong and get our rest. Can you go to sleep or do you want to hear a little more of our history?"

Maxter snuggled closer to Grandpa. "I'm big. I'm not sleepy. Please just tell me some more."

"Queen Cyberlina led the Internet in cooperation with the Council of the Minds. In the beginning, no single human or e-person ran the Internet alone. The Council worked together finding the best way for the Internet to help e-people and humans; it was an electronic democracy. This council was made up of human government and academic leaders, Cyberlina, her two sons, Algor and Henry, and one representative from the routers. This router was chosen in a vote by all the routers.

During this time, humans were embattled in a mighty war of words and ideas among many countries. The government representative to the Council feared that if another world war broke out, as had happened twice before, their lines of telephone communication might be destroyed. The Internet was designed to serve as their secret means of communicating. The Council gave Cyberlina the task of recruiting and training an exceptional top-secret squad of e-people called the Stealth Carriers."

Now the story was getting good. Images of dark secrets and sly, silent troops flashing through cyberspace on dangerous missions projected in Maxter's mind. Maxter thought of the downtrodden, laboring e-people he knew and couldn't imagine any of them being anything as cool as a Stealth Carrier might be. "So, Grandpa, who were the Stealth Carriers?"

"I was a Stealth Carrier," replied Grandpa, with more than a little pride in his voice. "We were selected by Cyberlina as the best young e-people in our land. Henry, who was just a prince at the time, wanted to be a Stealth Carrier, but Cyberlina selected Algor Ithum, his older brother, to represent the royal family in the force.

The selection process to become a Stealth Carrier was brutal. We had to be prepared to deliver our packets at warp speed in time of crisis. We learned strategies and tactics for moving about the Internet without being caught or without losing our packets. Cyberlina needed one Stealth Carrier Knight to be a representative on the Council of the Minds. It was a proud day for me to be voted to that position by my fellow Stealth Carriers. All the people who are now our family and closest neighbors were once Stealth Carriers or are descendants of the Stealth Carriers."

"What did all the other e-people do?" asked Maxter.

"All those who were not chosen to be Stealth Carriers became the Academic Carriers. They carried packets to many great professors and thinkers working out of universities. That's when our problems began. The Academic Carriers saw the Stealth Carriers with fast boards and representation on the Council of the Minds and they wanted a seat as well."

"That sounds fair. Everyone should have a seat," said Maxter.

"You're smart, Maxter, maybe they should have," answered Grandpa, "but that isn't what happened."

"What did happen?"

"As the Academic Carriers were growing restless, Henry was growing older. Being the youngest son, Henry knew he'd never be king. He felt doubly betrayed because Cyberlina had appointed Algor to the Stealth Carriers. He felt that he had no power at all. Ambitious Henry refused to accept this situation. Now, Henry is not the sort of man to earn power, or deserve power, so Henry plotted to take power. It so happened that right about the time that Henry was scheming for power, a new breed of humans were joining the Council of the Minds — the businessman. Some of the businessmen were good, trying to make the Internet better for the e-people and the humans. Others were just out for their own profit. One of the businessmen was my friend and teacher, Setag."

Looking at Maxter sitting beside him in rapt attention, E-Liam knew that he'd always be just rickety, old Grandpa to him. It seemed like just yesterday when he, E-Liam, bold Stealth Carrier Knight, and Setag, visionary young technologist, were launching ideas and stirring fierce debates in the Council of the Minds. The network that eventually brought the world to each human's home, evolved from those times. At heart, Grandpa was still that fearless young knight.

"Setag was a young man when he joined the Council and we became friends. Businesses by the hundreds were quickly joining governments and universities, flocking to use the networking and communication power of the Internet. Setag and I had great ideas about how the e-people and humans could work together to manage the ever-increasing amount of work, back-breaking workloads, looming on the horizon. Not everyone on the Council wanted to listen to the ideas of a young technologist and a Stealth Carrier.

The Council started to splinter into groups with

Setag and our new ideas on one side and the old-time Council members, Cyberlina and Algor, who wanted to keep things the same, on another. A third group, the most powerful and nasty faction, composed of Henry and the selfish businessmen all wanting to control the Internet for their own profit eventually squashed us all."

Growing sleepier, arms hugging his flannel pillow, Maxter asked, "How could Henry take over power if Algor was supposed to be the new king one day and he was a Stealth Carrier?"

"Henry hypnotized Algor, turning him into a babbling fool, ending his reign before it even began. Wanting to make sure that the code to break Algor from the trance was never said by accident, he made it "I love Olla."

"No one would ever say that," shot Maxter in disgust. That was nuts.

"Yes," chuckled E-Liam tousling Maxter's curly head. "This was a joke to himself because King Henry felt no one would ever love her — as creepy and disgusting as she was. Henry was certain this would keep Algor out of action forever. In his hypnotized state, all Algor could do was pace back and forth, repeating crazy phrases like claiming to have invented the Internet and such. Queen Cyberlina, now quite old, was heartbroken to see her youngest son, Henry, so evil. She was in enormous pain seeing her eldest son rendered useless, looking like a complete fool in his hypnotized state.

One night, toward the end of her great and caring life, she had a vision that one of her own beloved Stealth Carriers would bring forth a child. This child would become a great leader and restore the Council of the Minds, wrestling power away from Henry and his evil partners. She told Henry of her dream, telling him that his evil ways would end soon enough at the hands of a Stealth Carrier's child. That night she died of a broken heart. When the e-people heard of the death of the queen they loved and of her prophecy, they were stricken with grief, yet they had some hope. In a state of confusion and mourning they began their patient wait for their prophesied leader.

Henry was taking no chances. After his mother's vision, Henry decreed that all Stealth Carriers and their families were to live in a separate part of the Internet and would only have the slowest transport boards."

"So what was Henry's new Council like?" inquired Maxter. His eyes were growing heavy but he kept fighting sleep.

"The Council of the Minds was changed to the Control of Information Council which is still in power. The Control of Information is made up of King Henry and Olla, representing the e-people; an unscrupulous dot.com businessman; a censor-happy academic; and other unsavory characters representing the humans. Instead of being ruled by a democracy with its power in knowledge and choice, the e-people are ruled by fear: fear of Henry, fear of Olla and fear of the infestation.

Grandpa went on to describe the first infestation. "The bugs attacked us, blinding us with their wings, stopping our work, and crashing the systems. Algor reacted by chanting more than ever. Since King Henry could control Olla Brac it seemed like he was good, saving us from the bugs. Only he could make her stop the bugs. Because of that, the Academic Carriers believed at first that he was a strong and good ruler.

No Stealth Carrier or our descendants believed that one bit. It was the beginning of King Henry's terrible reign. That was his way of getting power over us. Before we knew what had happened Henry, Olla, her bugs and the Control of Information were the law of our land. We began our patient watch, waiting for the prophesied new leader to come."

E-Liam paused and looked over at Maxter. His tired little grandson was fast asleep.

✳

CHAPTER THREE

A Buggy Threat

The next day after school, E-Wally and Justin talked for hours. E-Wally told Justin more stories and legends about the e-people. Although delivering a huge daily assignment of e-mail sounded like backbreaking work, Justin couldn't help laughing at all the funny things E-Wally had seen while riding around on his cumbersome old transporter board.

"Is it like surfing when you ride that thing?" Justin asked, pointing to the bulky old board that E-Wally rode to deliver his e-mails.

"That's what we call it," answered E-Wally, surprised that Justin knew what surfing was. Justin surely didn't seem to need to do anything except use his keyboard to move around on the Internet. Suddenly feeling embarrassed by his sorry, old transport board, E-Wally added, "King Henry controls what boards e-people get. Some e-people deliver packets surfing on hyper transporter boards that are very fast. My family and everyone that lives near me have only been given these slow old boards to ride on," E-Wally said.

"That stinks. I love surfing. It's the coolest thing ever. You've gotta have the best equipment. Hang on, I'll find you a great board just like the one I wish I had. I've been wishing for this board for years and if I get straight A's I'll get fifty dollars. That's a good start on saving for it."

The thought of his previous good grades made Justin frown for a moment at the thought of the worksheet that sat incomplete in his book bag. Looks like science might be a D this grading period. But how many times does an e-person show up in a kid's hard drive? Justin shrugged off the nagging sense of concern and went on excitedly, "We can customize it to be really awesome."

Justin logged on to his favorite site www.Ronjons.com. He quickly copied a surfboard and some surfer clothes. In a flash he had opened up E-Wally's file and pasted everything into it. Then, Justin downloaded a virtual surfing game to teach E-Wally how to practice surfing on a real performance board.

"What are these for?" E-Wally asked, holding up the clothes Justin had gotten for him.

"Sorry E-Wally, but you can't be a surfer wearing a mailman uniform," Justin said, crinkling his nose at E-Wally's uniform. "Those are surfer clothes."

E-Wally tried on the baggy shorts, the wild red-flowered shirt, and the black sunglasses. He took off his e-delivery cap and tried on a baseball cap that had "No Fear" embroidered in bright blue letters.

"Now you're ready to surf," Justin said admiring the new look he'd given E-Wally. Justin remembered the first time he had gone surfing at Point Pacific. He had gotten a short board for his birthday last June. The early summer waves had been waist high and perfect. It was a day of wiping out, hard paddling, and lots of struggling to get even one decent ride. A new board is not an easy thing to master.

E-Wally had that same look he'd had that day. "I'm scared but I want to do this" was written all over his face. "Good luck, E-Wally, have fun!" Justin happily typed.

E-Wally gave Justin a little smile, straightened his shoulders, picked up his hyper transport board, and got ready to try balancing on it. He had seen other e-people surf the Internet on their sleek hypertext transport boards. He thought it looked about the same as riding his slow bulky board, only faster.

Boy, was E-Wally wrong. Surfing on this hyper transport board was hard. E-Wally couldn't even balance on it. He waved his arms and flopped his body back and forth trying to stay balanced. The board flipped and tipped. Time and time again E-Wally landed – oomph, on the ground. Finally E-Wally yelled out with glee, "I'm balancing! I've got it!"

"Now you're ready to play my favorite game. Lie down on the board and get ready for the first wave." With that, Justin started the Virtual Surfing Trainer program. E-Wally felt the hyper transport board move under him. Looking ahead at a sort of screen that Justin had imported to his file, E-Wally saw a virtual mountain of deep blue water rising on the horizon and on the screen a little cyber surfer guy ready to catch a wave.

"Oh bugs!" shouted E-Wally, his fingers white-knuckled as he gripped the edges of the board.

"Paddle!" shouted Justin. "Get moving and stand up when you catch the wave."

As the wall of water come closer, E-Wally paddled, watching the virtual image of himself moving on the screen ahead. Just as he felt his own board surge ahead, the cyber surfer on the screen did too. The next thing he knew he was flat on the ground. The little cyber surfer image on the screen was tumbling and gasping in powerful crunches of white water and foam.

"Stand up! You have to stand up when you get moving! That was the best wipeout I ever saw!" shouted Justin typing furiously, bouncing in his beanbag and shouting the words aloud as he typed. "When the wave moves you, stand up, balance, and keep moving to the right or left. Don't get caught in the breaking part of the wave. If you're going to help your grandpa, you're going to have to be fast so you'd better get the moves down right while you're here!"

E-Wally was really enjoying this adventure. Again and again, waves like the surging power of the Internet hit E-Wally, throwing him to the left and then to the right. He started to feel the right spot to stand on his hyper transport board so he could turn and stay balanced. One wave after another sent him flying off-balance on crashing virtual walls of water. It was difficult but E-Wally loved it!

After almost an hour of crushing waves and plenty of wipeouts, E-Wally hollered, "This is great. I can go so fast! Look at me turn!" It took only a slight shift in weight, a balance on his heels, and the board turned sharply left riding the face of the virtual wave. A grin spread from ear to ear as he exclaimed, "I never want to ride my bulky old board again! I wish my grandpa could see me on this." Remembering his grandfather made E-Wally suddenly sad.

Justin could see that E-Wally was upset "Hey, you were really bustin' some moves! What's wrong?"

How could E-Wally put it into words? This was the most fun he'd ever had. He was loving every minute of the surfing, the tree house, and playing with Justin. Maybe that was exactly the problem. "I'm having all this fun, it's the best. How come I'm feeling bad?" he wondered out loud.

"Are you worried about your grandpa?" asked Justin. "Do you miss your family?" Justin could easily imagine how it would feel to venture into some strange new world and miss your family even when the new world was amazing.

"Yeah, I really do," he replied nodding. A look of understanding passed between the two boys.

"What's your grandpa like?" Justin asked, really curious to hear all about the man who sounded more like a best friend than a grandpa.

E-Wally started to talk up a storm. It all rushed out in a homesick stream. He told Justin all about his grandpa, E-Liam. He told Justin the tales of the e-people that E-Liam used to tell E-Wally and his family as they spent many long evenings around the dinner table.

E-Wally explained how King Henry started the practice of giving e-people difficult assignments, forcing them to carry many packets a day. These assignments, called quotas, caused e-people to work long, tiring hours. To make things worse, King Henry ruled over all the routers on the Internet. The routers were so busy trying to handle the extra workload from Henry that they were mean and unhelpful to the poor overworked e-people. With all of the extra traffic in the Land of the Internet, the routers frequently had long lines called queues. Since each router only had room for a limited number of e-people and their packets in their queues, e-people frequently got bumped when the queues were full.

"I hate stuff like that," said Justin slapping the desk with his hand. "In our lunch room at school we have long lines almost every day. We have to wait and wait."

"It's worse than that," E-Wally explained. " When we get turned away by a router we don't just have to wait, we lose our packets. When a packet is lost we're forced to go back and get our packet from the server that sent it. We have to start all over again."

"Then why don't you just not wait in the line?" asked Justin.

"Are you crazy?" blurted E-Wally. "You obviously don't know a thing about fuzzball routers. They are these wild, fuzzy creatures that guard every route to every server. There is no way to get around them." Wondering if Justin was ready to hear even more about why e-people never, ever broke the laws, E-Wally continued. "King Henry knows when we break a rule, even the smallest of rules, and we are always punished."

"Oh," scoffed Justin. He lived with his little sister Ruthie who was always breaking the rules. "Don't tell me you never get away with anything."

"Hardly ever. We're punished by larger workloads or by some sort of hideous bug. We always get punished."

"Bugs?" Justin asked. He recalled all the times he had heard of computer bugs without ever thinking they were anything more than mere programming glitches. "What are you talking about?"

"There is this woman named Olla Brac who is King Henry's right-hand woman, the keeper and creator of all the bugs in the land. She is a gruesome and obese woman with a motley, black crew cut and giant streaks of blue over her eyes. She has an evil, wicked laugh that sounds like fingernails being dragged down a chalkboard. Sometimes we hear it when she's approaching, but usually we know when to run. She smells worse than week-old fish head garbage."

"That sounds really foul."

"Justin, you wouldn't believe the bugs infesting our land. King Henry is like a freak for game sites on the web. He used to visit them all the time and in one of his ventures he stumbled upon a gaming site where horrible morphed creatures had virtual battles every-day. That's where he met Olla Brac. Maybe he fell in love with her at first, or maybe he just wanted her to be a part of his evil plan to keep the e-people under his rule of terror, who knows. All we know is that King

Henry somehow enticed Olla to be his partner, to manage the bugs he brought to the Internet. We'll never know for sure.

He brought her to our land and she brought the bugs. Whenever she gets angry, which seems like all the time, she shakes her arm or flips her skirt and the bugs fly out. They're programmed to seek and destroy, to cause all sorts of trouble."

As Justin listened, he was amazed at his new friend. None of the kids at school ever seemed to get this serious about anything. It was cool to know someone near his own age that got intense about what mattered to him; he was ready to risk being caught by a horrible bug monster woman to save his grandpa.

E-Wally paused and looked straight into Justin's eyes, "I don't mind so much for me, it's my grandpa I worry about. He is so old and creaky, but he still gets on his transporter and delivers his entire e-mail quota every day just as fast as he can. Olla is set on getting rid of my grandpa just because he's old. She actually came to our house and stuck a warning note right on our door. That's the reason I ran away."

E-Wally's brow knit in concern as he remembered the angry way in which he had left home. He felt a giant twinge of pain tremor through his chest. It caught him off-guard for a minute, but then he continued. "Every night he looks more and more exhausted. Last Friday night Grandpa was telling a really funny story at dinnertime, but he was so exhausted that right in the middle of it his face plopped splat-down in his mashed potatoes."

Justin was listening so intensely to E-Wally's story that he did not hear the muffled sniff that came from under the bed. Ruthie had snuck into her brother's room right after dinner. Tonight she had brought her binoculars from her Girl Scout pack so she could read Justin's computer screen from under his bed. Ruthie wiped her runny nose on the corner of Justin's bedspread. She couldn't help crying just a little bit. That story was very sad and Ruthie just wanted to give poor Grandpa a hug or something.

"YOUR POOR GRANDPA!" typed Justin in bold capital letters.

"Now you see why I had to run away. I have to find a way to help my grandpa."

While Justin and E-Wally were talking, miles away, deep in the Land of the Internet, roars could be heard from the regal castle. There was a loud hollering coming from behind the gilded doors. A very short, wimpy-looking King Henry was pacing back and forth in the Control Room. "Find me Olla Brac!" his voice bellowed at its most authoritative volume, "Bring her to me now!"

King Henry was nearly bursting a gasket as he shouted at his humble servant, Sebastian. The shaking e-servant fled from King Henry's Control Room down the long, dank hall to find Olla Brac. He hated having to find Olla almost as much as he hated being yelled at by the king when he was in one of his moods. It wasn't that Olla was difficult to find; it was the smell. Rotten fish, sweaty old shoes, or an open sewer were all perfume compared to the stench of Olla.

"Oh," he moaned holding his stomach and his breath as he drew closer to her quarters. He didn't think she had ever bathed. Her bugs reveled in the stink — living up her sleeves, down deep in her pockets, and in the enormous black folds of her dress. As he turned the corner, he saw her right where he had expected her to be — sprawled on her lime green chaise. Her grotesque, blubberous folds oozed over the chaise's edges. She must have just popped one of her favorite treats, a huge Florida cockroach, into her mouth because one of its legs was still squirming in the corner of her mouth.

"Oh, your most honorable madam, the king requests you come to the Control Room immediately."

"Oh, he wants to see me, see me immediately," she said in her low husky voice. The body of the squirming bug that she had not yet swallowed muffled her words. "Yes, most certainly, immediately," she went on, patting her short, spikey, black hair to put it in place. She grunted indelicately while rising from her chaise and straightened her skirt.

"Umm, uhhh, madam," the e-servant said as he put

his finger to the corner of his mouth and made a slight sweeping motion, indicating that Olla might want to remove the unsightly cockroach leg from the corner of her mouth before her audience with the king.

"Oh, um, yes, of course" she said hastily, licking the leg from the corner of her mouth with her long, lizard-like tongue. Suddenly realizing that she had been told what to do by a mere e-person, she lividly spat out, "What are you waiting for? Stop dawdling," and bustled past him toward the Control Room. A flurry of small flying bugs formed a dark cloud swarming behind her, while multilegged creatures could be seen peeking out from under her sleeves and skirt.

"Good day, Henry. How fine you look in those rich indigo robes."

The sickeningly sweet way she greeted him in her fake high voice nearly made Henry toss his cookies.

"Have you been working out?" Olla said with a coy turn of her fat, rippling face.

"Hmmpf," began Henry evasively. Handling Olla's fascination with him took quick wit and a strong stomach. She was a force to be reckoned with and a valuable weapon in Henry's arsenal. Everything about her buggy, evil demeanor effectively kept e-people scared half out of their wits. Olla Brac was the reason e-people obediently pushed themselves to exhaustion, working the long hours his empire demanded.

While Henry found her repulsive, the feeling was not mutual. Olla adored Henry like a heart-sick puppy and filled his every request with a smile. The situation suited bitterly evil Henry just fine. He realized his own limitations. As frightening and powerful as Olla was, it was an entirely different story with Henry himself. It wasn't easy being short, even in his highest shoes, and on the thin side of scrawny. Even a cold heart and a wickedly conniving, power-hungry mind couldn't create an imposing figure out of King Henry. He did not look much like a king and he knew it. He had none of the political savvy and charm that served his mother, Queen Cyberlina, during her great rule. He had none of the appeal and quick, calculating intelligence of his brother, Algor. But Henry had what he needed. He had the lovesick Olla right under his thumb, right where he wanted her.

Clearing his throat in the most kingly fashion he could muster, Henry began to bring Olla up to speed on the latest runaway. "Another rebel has popped up from among the e-people. He's from the same family as that Anzwar scum."

"I was just out that way yesterday. Ha ha ha ha," she cackled, forgetting to be feminine and sweet in front of her idol, King Henry. "I gave E-Liam his last warning. He'll be in the null bin soon."

"Forget him," ordered King Henry impatiently. "You must get the word to each router to be on the watch for this runaway. I have no more details just yet. I want that e-person brought to me! He'll be dealt with severely."

"He's probably headed for the Outpost," announced Sebastian. It was well worth Henry's wrath to see the effect this statement always had on his squirrelly little face.

Without even glancing at the bearer of such irreverent news, Henry cuffed Sebastian, sending him rolling across the floor. Still in a heap, the e-servant smiled, it was one of his few joys to have brought a blanket of fear to the king's face. It was not a choice position, being servant to a weak, control freak of a king, but Sebastian knew the value of his post. All ears, quick and cunning, this e-servant had a purpose and the patience to carry it out. Most captured slaves serving in Henry's court felt doomed, destined to being stuck there for life; not this slave, not Sebastian.

Sebastian was startled out of his thoughts by a grating cackle. Unable to contain her delight at the thought of a capture for a moment longer, Olla Brac brusquely interrupted, "You have no worries, dear King." A broad wave of her hand sent bugs flying in every direction, and she cackled once again, "I will bring to you the runaway you describe. He'll not forget the power of my thousands of teeny, little bugs."

Holding his breath against her putrid smell, Henry

reached out his hand to walk Olla to the conference table. With her eyes goggling at the king, Olla took the seat next to Henry as they began to design their wicked plan. They would set every router on the alert. The routers would simply comply with the order, since they had no power or minds any more. They obeyed without argument since King Henry's control had rendered them droidlike zombies.

✳

Everything was not so under control at Justin's. Justin's mom knocked on his door. "Justin, lights out in ten minutes. I want you to show me your dinosaur assignment before bed. I'll come back after I tuck your sister in."

Justin freaked. "Oh my gosh, E-Wally, what am I going to do? I've been having so much fun with you that I forgot all about my stinky dinosaur project. My mom is going to kill me. I gotta go."

Amidst Justin's commotion, Ruthie sprang out from under the bed and dashed into her room just in time to be tucked in.

Justin ran to his book bag and grabbed his science folder. "Where is that worksheet?" he grumbled to himself as he tossed other papers aside. Ten minutes, how could he get it done in ten minutes?

When Justin found the worksheet that he was

looking for he logged onto the Internet and searched for "Dinosaurs." There were twenty-two empty spaces on his fill-in-the-blank worksheet. He used a search engine that searched through all of the websites in the Internet and showed Justin what it had found.

"There can't be 518 sites!" Justin yelled. "I can't go through 518 sites!"

Just then there was a knock on the door and Justin's mom came in.

"Well how did that dinosaur assignment turn out? I bet it wasn't as bad as you thought it would be."

"Well Mom, um, I well... you see... um," Justin stammered. He didn't know how to tell his mom that he'd barely even started it.

His mom did not say a word. She held out her hand to Justin for the paper. Justin handed it to her and looked down at his bare feet.

After a moment of silent disbelief his mother exploded, "Justin, you've barely even started! What on earth have you been doing up here for the last two nights?"

Justin did not say anything; he just kept looking at his feet. "I'm sorry Justin, but if you do not have this done by tomorrow afternoon, I'm going to have to take your computer away for good," his mom said. She put his assignment back on his desk and left his room.

CHAPTER FOUR

RUTHIE'S PLAN

From across the hall Ruthie tossed and turned under the blanket, tangling the sheets all around her legs. She had heard every bellowed word between her mom and Justin. Ruthie had not even had a chance to meet the strange computer boy Justin called E-Wally. Her doofy brother just couldn't lose his computer now. What could she do? One thing for certain was she could not allow herself to just fall asleep. Kicking the covers to the floor, Ruthie leaped from her bed and plopped onto the chair in front of her computer.

While it booted up she devised a plan. Minutes later Ruthie was in the darkened hall slowly pushing open Justin's bedroom door.

Justin had flung himself onto his bed and covered his head with his pillow. There was no way he wanted anyone to see him cry. Justin didn't even notice Ruthie slinking silently across his room. He was too upset. It was hopeless. Even if he started looking through the 518 dinosaur sites right now, he would still not finish by tomorrow. If he lost his computer, he'd never see E-Wally again.

Meanwhile, another boy was crying in Justin's room — E-Wally. Justin had not closed the file that E-Wally lived in, so E-Wally had heard everything Justin and his mom had said. E-Wally was scared. What if Justin's mom took away his computer? He'd be stuck in the hard drive forever. It terrified E-Wally to think he might not be able to return home or find a way to save his grandpa.

Before E-Wally could think of what to do, a tousle of curls and two big brown eyes peered into the screen in front of him. "Hi," she typed, " I'm Ruthie. I'm Justin's little sister. I know all about you, and you better go find a way to help my brother or you'll be in a mess."

Taken back by the torrent of words and the new face peering into his file, E-Wally asked, "How can I help him?" as he rushed to wipe the tears from his face, embarrassed to be caught crying like an e-baby.

"You are Justin's only hope. Now listen. I don't care if my brother gets in trouble...well, maybe a little bit, but mostly I think you are so cool. Anyway, I have a plan," and with that she slid a diskette into the drive and opened a Paint file. With a few clicks on the keyboard she copied a picture of a small green and brown baby T-Rex and pasted it into E-Wally's file. The tiny T-Rex let out a raspy roar and showed E-Wally her sharp teeth. The little T-Rex looked curiously up at E-Wally, who jumped backwards with a start. He had never seen a creature that looked like that before!

"Hey, E-Wally," said Ruthie. " Don't worry. She's just a baby. But she's the kind of creature you'll be looking for out on the Internet. If you look for something like her I know you'll find a web site that'll give Justin the answers to his worksheet."

"I can't go on web pages. I'm scared! First of all I'm a runaway, and the fuzzball routers will be looking for me. Second, it is against the law of my land. I can't go onto web pages," he answered, shaking his head and closing his eyes tightly against the vision of what would happen to him if he were to be caught. "Besides, there must be some other way."

"I've been watching you practice on the Virtual Surfing Trainer. You mastered 'Crusher Pipeline,' the top level. I know you can surf past any stupid router," insisted Ruthie. " You were brave enough to run away and come here. How will you ever be brave enough to go back to save your poor grandpa if you don't help out my brother?"

It was hard for anyone to argue with Ruthie, and E-Wally's fear was no match for her determination. He wondered how this new human knew so much about him. While E-Wally was trying to figure out what to do, the baby T-Rex had scampered over to the tree and examined the rope swing. Suddenly she jumped straight up and grabbed the thick rope with her sharp little teeth, shaking it wildly, like a rambunctious puppy. E-Wally took in the whole scene and couldn't help but let out a big belly laugh. Perhaps finding the dinosaurs wouldn't be so bad after all.

E-Wally knew that Ruthie was right. He had mastered the Virtual Surfing Trainer. Most importantly, E-Wally knew he had to help his friend Justin.

Luckily Justin had not logged off the Internet, so E-Wally grabbed his sleek hyper transport board and took one last deep breath. E-Wally cruised out from Justin's computer, surfing quickly into the Land of the Internet. "Whoa!" shouted E-Wally. Being out in the buzzing, humming wires with a super-fast transport board was much more difficult than the Virtual Surfing Trainer game. E-Wally's red flowered shirt rippled in the wind caused by his abrupt sharp turn out of the server. He held his arms wide to each side for balance as he turned and twisted through the lines with his left sneakered foot perched close to the nose

of the board. His right foot was planted firmly just behind the center. It rocked, tilting the board for pin-
point steering. He surfed like a pro, whizzing by the
lines of e-people carrying their heavy packs on their
old heavy boards. E-Wally was amazed at how fast he
was traveling.

Speeding past many e-people on the less traveled
routes near Justin's computer, E-Wally saw a NAP in
the distance, an entranceway to the Internet Highway.
He smirked, remembering how scared he used to be
to pass through the NAP and enter the Highway. E-
people on faster boards used to speed by him and cut
him off. Now he had the fastest board and no one
would be cutting him off.

E-Wally cruised up to the NAP, adjusted his backwards cap, felt the embroidered words "No Fear,"
and held in his breath sharply. "That's right, no fear
– here I goooooo." He blasted off onto the highway with
a burst of speed.

The highway was jammed with e-people carrying
their heavy packets. Disappointed, E-Wally soon had
to slow down to avoid slamming into a burly e-person just ahead of him. "Oh, man!" he mumbled impatiently, since he just wanted to find the dinosaur
website and get back to Justin's computer as fast as
possible. Even though E-Wally had a fast board, he
could not speed along as he had hoped. The highways
had grown more and more crowded over the past

years. It seemed like every day the Information High-way, as some called it, grew more and more crowd-ed as more and more humans sent and requested in-formation packets.

E-Wally eyed the traffic ahead of him and spied an opening in the middle lane. Using the skills he mas-tered on the Virtual Surfing Trainer he maneuvered his way from one opening to another, weaving his way down the line. Router to router E-Wally traveled, passing by the routers who did not know him. Quick-ly E-Wally approached the router that was closest to the website. It was the last router leading into some frightening place where a dinosaur creature lived. This was the moment that he dreaded and feared. He rubbed his hand over the back of his hat again. "No fear, no fear," he repeated to himself.

When he arrived at the router's line he looked up at the giant routing table on the wall. It blinked with yellow lights, looking much like the schedules in a train station. Instead of displaying information humans need, such as which gate to go to to catch the west-bound train, the routing table gave the e-people all the numbers they needed about the routes they'd take to deliver their packets.

The long queue of e-people moved slowly toward the exit, giving E-Wally all the time he needed to lo-cate the route he would take to get to the ZoomDi-nosaurs.com web site he was aiming toward. E-Wally swallowed hard, and his heart was pounding wildly in his chest as he drew nearer to the router. Thinking of the long, flowing hair that covered the router from head to knees, he hoped the router's eyes were covered enough to miss the fact that E-Wally was out of uniform.

Routers were almost all hair with skinny arms, knobby knees, and large-toed feet. E-Wally nervously laughed to himself remembering the chant all little e-kids sang about the routers:

> Fuzzball, fuzzball,
> Trip on your hair,
> We don't care,
> Get out of our way,
> Make our day,
> Fuzzball, fuzzball.

As they waited, the other e-people balanced easily on their thick, long boards, but E-Wally's hyper transport board was light and small. Knowing that the wait would be long, E-Wally kicked up his board and leaned it against his shoulder. He glanced up the line to see how many people were ahead of him.

E-people headed to routers all day and night. If a router didn't keep the traffic flowing there was a huge traffic jam. When routers were slow, like this fuzzball router was, e-people arriving after the queue was full were cut off the line. According to King Henry's rules, each queue could only hold a certain number of e-people. This queue held seven and there was no waiting around once seven were in line. Once they were cut off, they lost their packets. As soon as a packet was lost, the e-person had to return all the way back to their original server to retrieve them again. Even though this process happens in split seconds in human time, it means a ton of work for an e-person. It means starting the delivery all over again.

E-Wally's angry eyes scanned the queue, counting one, two, three, four, five. There were already five people in line with the limit set at seven. Another crowd of e-people was approaching and many would be turned away, losing their packets and having to start their deliveries all over again. This is what slowed poor Grandpa down so often.

The e-man in front of E-Wally passed through the router's gate, leaving E-Wally next in line. Like laser beams, his eyes focused on the wild hairiness of the slow, unseeing, heartless router mechanically checking off e-people. That fuzzball was oblivious to the pain he was inflicting. E-Wally remembered all the nights after long, backbreaking days of work when he'd been turned away at this slow queue.

Rage began to boil in E-Wally. It was a rage he had never felt before; it erupted from his heart like hot lava and scattered the butterflies from his stomach and filled every inch of his body. He felt no more fear, only rage. His hands grasped his board so tightly that his knuckles turned white. Without a thought for routine or procedure E-Wally leaped on his board and started wildly circling the router, wind whistling in his ears. Cutting a sharp turn, E-Wally stopped nose to nose in front of the router. With one voice the entire queue let out a gasp.

"Hey there fuzzball, have you missed me?" he taunted. "Haven't been able to check me off your little list have you?" The fuzzball router whirled his head toward E-Wally. The router realized that this was the runaway Olla was looking for.

"You fuzzball, you want to keep this line slow? I'll show you slow." With that E-Wally spun eight more dizzying turns around the router. Stopping once again, his board nearly rapped the router on the nose. "I don't have to wait in your line anymore."

In a confused fog of hair and surprise, and not a small amount of fury, the router reached out to grab E-Wally, dropping his check-pad in the process. He was no match for the speeding e-boy now frantic with adrenaline. Deftly whipping up his ratty hank of hair with one hand, the router finally had a clear view of this rebellious, young e-boy.

The skirmish escalated, attracting the attention of every e-person in the vicinity. Squinting to see what was going on, the sixth person in the queue suddenly turned to the e-boy behind him and said, "Pete, isn't that your friend up there?"

Pete stretched himself up to his full height, balanced on tiptoes, and craned his neck to look ahead where all eyes were focused. Although the boy was wearing odd and foreign clothes that Pete had never before seen, it was indeed his best friend, E-Wally. A strange mix of pride and trepidation filled Pete at the sight of his buddy bravely battling the router. Pete soon had a closer look when the queue began to move quickly forward. E-Wally had distracted the router so that he had moved away from his post. In a flood, the e-people poured through the port onto their desired routes. Seven, then fourteen, then dozens and dozens of e-people were on their way. Pete let many pass him by, hypnotized by the sight of E-Wally buzzing about the frustrated router. Pete gaped in awe at E-Wally's maneuvers on his hyper transport board. *What's going on? Where'd E-Wally come from and where'd he get that Hyper Transport board?* Pete wondered. Afraid to shout to his friend for fear he'd distract E-Wally, Pete was barely breathing in his nervous excitement. E-Wally exuded a confidence and bravery not seen in e-people since the beginning of the tyrannical rule of King Henry.

But Pete's fascination turned quickly to worry. If E-Wally was captured by the fuzzball router, he would be sent directly to Olla Brac. That evil woman would feed him to her bugs or send him off to work on the chain gang doing streaming video. *Why is he risking his life like this?* Pete's stomach churned as his eyes stayed locked on his wildly zooming best friend.

E -Wally and the fuzzball router's darting duel took them further and further into the dark, galactic void of the router container until they were mere specks. When Pete could no longer see them, he carried his own packet through the port joining the jubilant e-people on their routes.

Back in the dark router container a whirling, spinning match was still being fought. E-Wally tried to show some confidence. "Give it up you miserable troll," he said as the gawky, uncoordinated router batted away at him with long, bony arms.

In a voice that had the shrillness of scraping metal, the fuzzball router threatened loudly, "You're mine, you insolent rebel. No little squirt e-boy on a fancy board will disrupt my queue. Olla will love me for catching you." The router was propelled by some invisible whirlwind force. With scraggly hair streaming back close to his body, he made a grotesque sight honing in on E-Wally. Spinning faster and faster E-Wally dodged the router until he felt dizzy. When E-Wally paused to gain his bearings, he saw a totally unfamiliar scene, far from the familiar queue.

E-Wally had never actually spent much time in a

router. His entire life had been waiting in a queue, getting permission to enter the port and speeding out onto the correct route. Surfing through an unknown area, E-Wally was disoriented. Metal walls on all sides were broken up by a series of ports. Here and there weak lights from the router tables broke the darkness. Suddenly E-Wally was knocked to his knees as the fuzzball hammered him in the chest, ramming him with a forceful head butt.

The fuzzball careened to the left. E-Wally took that opportunity to gather back his breath and scramble to his feet. A cold sweat broke out over his entire body, and he felt shaky. Looking for a power surge, any wave that could give him some speed, E-Wally carved a sharp turn to the right and prepared to drive the fuzzball out of the router and into the safe light of day. Spinning back to face E-Wally, the router let out a bellow. His hair was snarled, wrapped tightly around his body, and his hands were clenched in angry fists. "Prepare to be captured," the router yelled with furious confidence as he began a turbulent spiral toward E-Wally.

The years of frustration drove E-Wally into a fury. He caught a power surge and lured the router into a dizzying pursuit. Winded, the router paused for a moment, panting and confused. E-Wally took that brief opportunity to scan the cavernous cube for an open port. Suddenly the router was on him. E-Wally stopped short in surprise and whirled around with his fists flailing. With a quick reach of his long arms, the fuzzball grabbed the backwards brim of E-Wally's baseball cap, cackling out a laugh laced with cold hatred. "I've got you now," he said as he grabbed at E-Wally with his one free hand. Startled, E-Wally ducked down, out and away from his cap, and sped forward, never looking where he was going. He had to get away. Holding his breath, E-Wally traveled through a dark, unmarked portal. Once on the other side, he realized he was on a regular line, heading straight toward the dinosaur site.

E-Wally, the rebel e-boy, shot through the last line, his red-flowered shirt flapping wildly behind him, "I did it!" He threw back his head and joyfully sang out, "Fuzzball, Fuzzball."

Crouching deftly, he maneuvered along the wires to the dinosaur site. All of a sudden E-Wally realized that he was going so fast that he couldn't stop himself. Smack! With a bang he crashed right into the snout of a giant T-Rex. With a start the T-Rex let out a mighty sneeze, sending E-Wally rolling to the ground covered with giant, slippery, green snot.

"Ahh!" E-Wally screamed as he tried to pull himself out of the stinky guck that was sticking to his arms and legs in long stretchy bands.

"Rrrrrrraahhhhh!" the giant, old dinosaur bellowed swinging his gigantic, scaly brown head down to see what had hit him. A dollop of drool fell from his tremendous mouth, splattering like a giant water balloon beside E-Wally. He looked up in time to see two rows of fangs clamp shut. Just when E-Wally thought that he was going to be a dino-snack, the giant T-Rex started to laugh. He laughed so hard that the ground shook, and poor E-Wally bounced up and down like a ball — through the snot, into the slobber, and finally free of both. As E-Wally tried to stand up, wiping the disgusting liquids from his face, he thought that Ruthie had certainly tricked him with her cute little microscopic dinosaur. This T-Rex was terrifying.

"What do we have here?" asked the dinosaur with his tremendous head cocked to the side. He had a slow and gentle voice. E-Wally did not answer. "Well, do you speak?" the dinosaur asked again. Each time he spoke, E-Wally was hit with a fresh wave of hot and humid dino breath.

Even though the dinosaur sounded nice, E-Wally was too scared to speak. He just nodded his head.

"Well, if you speak, speak boy. Who are you?"

"E-Wally," he finally replied. He was growing confident in the fact that he was not going to become a dinosaur snack.

"Well E-Wally, you can call me T."

T lay down next to E-Wally. With T lying down, he looked a lot less humongous to E-Wally.

"So E-Wally, what brought you into our museum?"

"My friend is in trouble."

"What kind of trouble?" T asked, raising his leathery reptilian brow.

E-Wally explained to T how Justin had saved him and helped him learn to surf. He told T that Justin needed a dinosaur to help him with his assignment so he wouldn't lose his computer.

As E-Wally was telling T his story, a small reptile joined them. He was about as long as E-Wally was tall, with bright green skin that was much smoother than T's. Even though he stretched his short neck out as long as it could go, he only came up to E-Wally's chest. E-Wally did not know what it was, but it looked familiar.

"Who's the new guy?" asked the creature in a cocky, deep voice, trying to be more intimidating than his short stature made him appear.

"This is E-Wally. E-Wally, this is my cousin, Theodore," said T.

"You're cousins? Why are you so small and T is so big?" E-Wally thought it would take at least a hundred Theodores to make one T.

"Small? Small? I'll show you small!" Theodore screamed, fanning a bright red bulge out of his neck as he jumped on all four of his squatty little legs and tried to put his face in E-Wally's.

At the sight of Theodore's exploding neck, E-Wally jumped behind his surfboard. T laughed at his cousin's typical overreaction and then explained, "Now the first thing you have to learn around here is that Theo is a bit sensitive about being so much smaller than the rest of the family; it's better not to bring it up."

E-Wally peered out from behind his board. Theo had relaxed and his neck was back to normal. While taking a closer look at Theo to make sure that his neck, or any other part of his body, was not going to ex-plode again, E-Wally realized that he did look familiar. He thought for a moment. "Oh yeah, Jimmy," he said quietly. "My friend Justin has a pet named Jimmy that looks a lot like you," he explained, hoping that Theo would be friendly.

"Well now, if your friend has a reptile pet, then he already knows a lot about dinosaurs. He probably just doesn't realize it. Maybe Theo and I need to take a trip with you to go see Justin."

"Really! Do you mean it?" E-Wally exclaimed, jumping excitedly from behind his board.

"Sure, let's go," T said, and with a low grunt he lumbered slowly off the ground. Straightening his hind legs first, he raised his tremendous backside and then raised his head and neck with his tree-like front legs.

E-Wally, Theo, and T carefully traveled back through the Internet — past the routers, through the server, and back into Justin's computer. The moment Ruthie saw them arrive she let out a scream and clapped her hands with glee. In the midst of all this commotion, Justin woke up and saw his sister sitting at his desk. "What's going on Ruthie? Why are you in my room?"

Looking at his monitor, Justin noticed that E-Wally was sitting on the back of a giant T-Rex. He rubbed his eyes in confusion and asked again, "What's going on Ruthie?" With pride, Ruthie pulled Justin out from under his covers and dragged him over to the desk. He sat down and immediately started typing, "What's going on E-Wally?" Now he was wide awake, eyes huge in wonder.

"Your sister told me to go find a dinosaur to help you with your assignment. She drew me that one so I would know what to look for," E-Wally explained, pointing to the baby T-Rex. "She was a little off on the size though," E-Wally finished with a humph.

"What? You went to a web page? You traveled past routers? How did you do it without getting caught?" Justin's flood of awe and disbelief was cut short by Theodore.

Theodore leaped off the back of T and ran over to the baby T-Rex. "Who is this guy?" Theodore questioned arrogantly, looking down his pointed green nose.

Ruthie elbowed her brother and snatched the keyboard out of his hands, "What do you mean, who's this guy," Ruthie replied indignantly. "She's Xena, my baby T-Rex. I drew her for E-Wally."

"She doesn't look much like a T-Rex to me. You made her look like Jimmy, my pet Iguana" Justin taunted, not appreciating the sharp elbowing one bit.

"She doesn't look anything like Jimmy. She is a T-Rex," retorted Ruthie. She glanced at the aquarium filled with tropical plants and the green iguana named Jimmy. T-Rex looked over too.

"Hey guys, you're both right," T said, ending their argument. "You think they look the same because we're all one big family. Justin, E-Wally told me you are in big trouble with your mom. We are here to teach you about dinosaurs. Spend some time with Theo and me and you'll be able to answer any questions your teacher gives you."

T-Rex told Justin to go get Jimmy and bring him over to the desk. Justin went to the warm lit aquarium and lifted off the screen top. He gently reached in and picked up the iguana, waking Jimmy from a deep sleep. The brownish green lizard rolled open one of his beady, black eyes to see what his owner was doing with him at this odd hour. "Let's see how much you already know," T said when Justin and Jimmy appeared in front of the computer screen.

"I don't know anything," whined Justin. "I've only answered three of the questions on my worksheet and I have twenty-two left."

"We'll see about that. I suspect you know more than you think." T asked Justin to look closely at Jimmy's skin, claws, and the shape of his legs and head. "Now take a close look at me."

Justin stared at Jimmy for a long moment and then looked hard at T-Rex.

"This is so cool. I have my own tiny dinosaur," Justin declared.

"Don't say ..." E-Wally tried to stop Justin, but it was too late.

"Tiny? Tiny? You think I'm tiny?" Theo rammed his head into Justin's computer screen and flared the bright red bulge out of his neck. Ruthie and Justin simultaneously jolted back from the monitor fearing that the computer screen was going to explode at any moment. E-Wally and T just looked at each other and laughed.

After they had settled Theo down, Justin, T, and Theo talked about all of the iguanas' and dinosaurs' similarities and differences. Jimmy's diet, his skin, the shape of his feet, and the way he moved suddenly became exciting and new when Justin realized how many things his pet had in common with a tyrannosaurus rex. T got a bit sad when he explained about his ancestors becoming extinct, but then he made them all laugh with a story about a grouchy pterodactyl named Cyrus.

Justin was stuck on a question about dinosaur bones and how scientists figure out what animal they have found by identifying the bones. "Wait, look at my website. There's a game there that will help you understand." Justin quickly pulled up the website as T instructed. The game was great. It was a giant puzzle using dinosaur bones as pieces. The game began with a large color picture showing an outline of a T-Rex. Justin and Ruthie loved finding a way to drag and drop, eventually putting all the bones in the right place.

"Remember when you broke your collarbone on your skateboard, Justin?" reminded Ruthie, running to Justin's closet and pulling out a big tan envelope.

"Oh yeah, I have pictures of my bones in there. I wonder if my bones look like T's?" Justin held a large x-ray next to the monitor. "Whoa, look at that. My ribs are all puny and we don't even have the same number of ribs. Look at the size of my shoulder blades compared to those mega-things in T's back."

T took a look at the x-ray. "Sure, Justin. You might not know this, but birds are descendants of dinosaurs. Those large bones tell scientists that some dinosaurs probably had wings millions of years ago," explained T-Rex, leaning toward Justin and Ruthie until his greenish, smiling face filled the entire monitor screen. The night flew by as T and Theo helped Justin discover answers to all his questions. Justin created a chart for his science class that showed all the similarities and differences between dinosaurs and iguanas. He printed out pictures of T and other dinosaurs and reptiles.

Soon Justin's room filled with the warm, orange light of the rising sun. For once the kids were not dragging slowly out of bed; instead they were eager to get to the bus. Ruthie ran to get her book bag and raced back to Justin's room. Justin gathered his stuff and put Jimmy back into his cage.

"Thanks E-Wally," said Justin, who was promptly given a sly nudge by Ruthie. "Oh, sure, and you too, Ruthie, for getting T and Theo. You saved me!" Justin reached over and playfully tousled his little sister's curls. Ruthie batted away her brother's hand as a warm pink color rose to her cheeks. It wasn't every day that her big brother gave her a compliment like that.

"I owed you one. See you after school," E-Wally replied with a wink.

Justin grabbed his book bag and Jimmy's cage and headed downstairs to show his mom what he had learned. "Mom! Mom! Where are you? I have the coolest thing to show you."

"Good morning, Justin," his mom said when he found her in the kitchen. "Slow down. What are you so excited about?"

"Dinosaurs are way cool! Here look."

Justin showed his mom the pictures of T and explained all the things he had taught Justin. Of course he left out the fact that he had actually been talking to the dinosaurs in his computer. Justin's mom was so proud of him. She gave him a giant hug, so tight that he thought she might even squish him!

At school Justin's teacher was glad to have the hardworking Justin back. For weeks Justin had been barely awake during her lectures on dinosaurs. She pondered the sudden change in her entire class as Justin demonstrated all the things he had learned. Each of his classmates took a turn holding Jimmy.

Justin's best friend Steven was just glad that they had one class period without a boring lecture. "Amazing," whispered Steven to himself. "She's more excited about Justin's Dino/Iguana chart than she is about him getting all the worksheet questions right."

All year Steven had waited for one fun science class. It was about time. Steven cared about only one thing — growing up and being a scientist. Maybe he would do something cool like Justin did; maybe Mrs. Restrepo would let him teach a class his way too.

While Justin was at school, E-Wally was thinking of his adventures from the night before. That fuzzball had been quick, strong, and really angry. E-Wally ran his hand over the smooth edge of his board as he thought about his grandpa. His grandpa was the reason he was here, wasn't he? Finding a way to help his grandfather was the reason he had dared to run away in the first place. E-Wally started to pace back and forth in front of his tree house. He had been brave enough to run away, brave enough to go past the servers. He had mastered high levels of the Virtual Surfing Trainer.

E-Wally thought about his adventure with T and the website. *I risked getting caught to help Justin, now I have to be brave enough to go home and get Grandpa.* E-Wally figured Grandpa E-Liam could live in Justin's hard drive forever, resting happy and free of King Henry's mountainous workloads and Olla Brac's terrible punishments.

E-Wally kicked at the end of his tree house slide. *Who am I kidding? Yeah sure, like I'll just surf on up to my house and grab Grandpa,* he thought bitterly. Getting Grandpa back to Justin's computer was going to be a hundred times more dangerous and difficult than finding T.

Now that I've fought one router, all of them will be on the lookout for me. They'll know what I look like and what I'm wearing. I have to make it home or things will be a thousand times worse for Grandpa and my whole family, worried E-Wally, pacing round and round the base of the tree while Xena hopped merrily along behind him.

✴

CHAPTER FIVE

THE CAVERN OF OLLA BRAC

In the Control Room of the royal palace where King Henry and Olla were meeting again, tension splintered the air.

"So, you caught the e-boy and things are perfect," Henry said with one hand casually draped over his nose against her ghastly smell.

"I did everything you asked, but things are not perfect, dear King," cooed Olla.

Henry's head whipped around and he glared

piercingly into Olla's squinty eyes. "What do you mean, things are not perfect?"

"That runaway, rebel e-boy's still on the loose and he's broken ranks in an even more serious manner. He battled a fuzzball router yesterday." Pulling E-Wally's baseball cap from the folds of her bug-splattered, filthy gown, Olla said, "The router that brought me this trophy should have caught the truant e-boy yesterday, but he let the wily little runt get away. The boy's out of uniform, he hasn't been working, and he's stolen some type of hyper transport board." She shoved the "No Fear" cap proudly toward Henry.

Henry clamped his mouth down tight, his jaw clenched in rage. The muscles in his face flexed, his cheeks flamed, and his eyes narrowed in thought. He grabbed the hat from Olla. Staring at the strange hat, he paced across the room and back again, boots hammering out a harsh rhythm. "Here, take this hat back. What do I want with it?" he spat at Olla, tossing the hat toward her feet. "Find that weasely runt. I want to talk to him. I've got a punishment worse than death. Bring him back to me alive."

Olla nodded gleefully. The desperate look on Henry's face made her feel needed and important. "I can work all night," pledged Olla, proud to play an important role in Henry's wicked plan. "By midday tomorrow I'll deliver you the means to capture the rebel boy, and I will not fail like your droid fuzzball did."

"Fine. Good-bye," said Henry with no further ado.

Ignoring Henry's curt dismissal, Olla flittered, "Don't you worry, O dear King. I'll get him. He's just a little fly in the ointment. I'll get him. Don't you worry." *Who is this little brat? No one gets away from the routers.* The thought of this little rebel made her stomach churn, and she just couldn't let this kid make her look bad in front of the king.

Henry was finished with this meeting. News of the rebel e-boy turned his stomach, already nauseated by Olla. If she didn't leave soon he was going to get downright sick. "Okay, Okay, just create your buggy plan," Henry replied, drawing the corner of his indigo cape in front of his face to mask the odor. "And do it quickly," he added as he motioned to the nearby e-servant with a small sweep of his hand to get Olla out of the Control Room.

"Oh yes, quickly, quickly, I will do it quickly." Olla tried to come up with something clever to say, something interesting so she could prolong her visit with the king, but her slow wit left her without words and she was prodded gingerly out of the room by Sebastian and a dozen of the king's other e-servants. Once they got her past the doorway, two e-servants swiftly drew the doors closed to keep her from trying to re-enter the Control Room.

The great doors slammed shut with an echoing thud, narrowly missing her bulbous nose, and stirring a blizzard of fleas, flies, and gnats from her robes. "Well, good-bye then," she mumbled to the door, once again speaking in her natural baritone voice. With a lumbering turn she headed back to her quarters. *I'll go straight to The Cavern*, she thought to herself as she clutched the baseball cap tightly in her hand. The very thought of this little rebel who defied Henry's laws made her mad. No, it made her fume. She tightened her grip on the hat as she thundered down the corridor. E-servants fled for cover as she approached them, diving into doorways and pressing themselves flat against the hall walls. Her labored breathing made her sound like a raging bull entering a ring. Olla rarely moved faster than a slug, so her current pace warned the nearby e-servants to take no chances.

With one violent motion, Olla threw open the gray slate door to The Cavern — her prized bug laboratory. This was the place where she created and kept her most horrible creations. Her beady, black eyes scanned the dark rock walls. In the walls were alcoves of various sizes holding hives, nests, webs, and colonies of countless species and their mutants. There were beehives made of mud and straw as large as watermelons jutting out from the jagged walls. Gray, domed wasp nests hung throughout The Cavern from the mildewy ceiling like decorative chandeliers.

Olla ran her hands along the smooth glass of an

aquarium. Some of her creations, especially her mutants, were contained in aquariums to keep them from eating the Cavern's other inhabitants. Like puppies nudging their owner for attention, the fire ants in the glass cage clamored to the glass where Olla's hand was placed. "Not today, my dears, not today," she cooed at them.

No, although their sting was torturous and, in a swarm, even deadly to an e-person, they would not be fast enough for this e-boy and his now infamous maneuverability. Olla continued around the cavelike room, checking on her critters and creations. The termites were busy adding on to their nest, which now towered over Olla's head to a staggering height. The lice hopped up and down happily on their furry perch while the roaches feasted on an afternoon snack.

Watching the roaches eat stirred Olla's stomach to a low, rumbling growl. *A snack, perhaps I'll fix myself a little refreshment*, she thought. The cool, moist darkness of the room had a calming effect on Olla. Relaxing, she surveyed her surroundings for the perfect snack. Her eyes fell on her favorite. With a swift hand she plucked six plump black cockroaches off the damp wall. Perched on a nearby black and gray marbled table was a shiny steel contraption. It was the only place in the Cavern where not a single bug could be found — well, a single whole bug, that is. After lay-ing the cockroaches one by one on the contraption's conveyer belt, Olla began to crank the long handle. Her anger and fury of just a few minutes earlier faded. A smile slowly crept across her face at the crunching and oozing sounds coming from the metal machine. The belt with the cockroaches on it fed the mouth of the machine, which smushed, crunched, and pummeled the bugs. Olla placed a glass at the opposite end of the machine and waited in happy anticipation. Out from the machine flowed a stream of cold white roach blood. Grasping the glass in her eager hand she brought it to her nose and deeply inhaled. "Ahh," she gushed with delight, "freshly squished cockroach juice, what a treat."

Over the marble table towered an apothecary cabinet made of small drawers and glass-doored cabinets, each the size of a mouse. Each of the drawers and cabinets held a vile or bottle of one of her creature's blood or venom. Each day Olla drank the blood and venom of one of her bugs to keep her immune to their deadly bites. "Which one today, which one today," she pondered as she lightly fingered the drawers with her free hand. After some quick deliberation, she selected a cobalt blue, pear-shaped bottle.

She uncorked the bottle and swirled its contents: the blood of the blue death beetle, one of her most effective creations. When let loose the beetle's lethal blue venom is deadly to e-carriers. At the same

time it is most annoying to humans, since it caus-
es the phenomenon of the "blue screen of death." The
blue screen of death is a fatal error that forces the
human to reboot the computer; it frequently results
in losing unsaved work. Olla cautiously dropped
three drops of the venom into her glass and swirled
the cocktail with a turn of her wrist. It was ready.
With the speed of a lightening bolt, her lizardlike
tongue shot out of her cavernous mouth as she
greedily slurped up her tasty treat.

Having satisfied her craving for a treat, it was
time for Olla to get down to work and figure out a way
to catch that rebel e-boy and bring him to King
Henry. Olla always did her best thinking in the bathtub. She just loved to lounge in the cool water and pon-
der her next terrible creation or solve her latest problem. Olla threw her robes onto her chair, upsetting
the fleas, flies, and gnats that lived in the robes and
creating a flurry of wings. She held on to a nearby
rock as she lowered her huge blubbery body into the
water. Olla's bathtub was not like a normal person's
tub for two reasons: the water and the bugs. Since Olla
had moved into the castle ten years ago, she had never
changed her bathtub water. It had changed from clean
and clear, to dirty yellow, to stinky and brown to thick
green slimy muck. The bugs, especially the mosquitoes, loved Olla's swamplike tub almost as much as
she did. The mosquitoes formed a thick cloud over the

tub, and Olla thought it gave her bath a lovely atmosphere. She also loved the loud humming that the hundreds of flying bugs created.

Olla sat on the bottom of the tub and let the thickest of the slime, which coated the top of the water, cover her shoulders like a green, furry, velvet cloak. Olla reached out of the tub to grab the rebel boy's hat. She held the hat close to her face. *Where would a poor e-delivery boy get an odd hat like this?* "No Fear," she read from the brim of the hat. So the boy thought he had no fear. She would design a plan that he would fear. Her plan would have to be clever enough to locate him and fast enough to stop him when he was found.

She didn't want to kill him, so fatal venom was not an option. King Henry wanted the boy returned to the castle alive. Once he was brought before the king, a fitting punishment would be decided upon.

Maybe the king will ask me for my opinion. Olla practiced how she would respond to the king in such an unlikely situation. "Oh, my opinion. You want to know what I would do?" she practiced in her fake feminine voice. Olla would, of course, recommend a life sentence to the streaming gangs. Olla barked a wicked laugh at the thought of sending an e-boy who was bold enough to wear a "No Fear" hat to the streaming gangs.

"You will have a lot to fear boy — a lifetime of fear," she said out loud to the hat, as if E-Wally was wearing it there in her swampy bathtub.

Henry had created the streaming gangs a few years back at the request of his human friends. The humans wanted a way to provide humans with chat rooms and streaming video requiring info packets to be delivered one after the next without delay. E-people who delivered their packets slowly or dared to run away were sentenced to the gangs. The sentenced e-people were chained together and forced to work nonstop without food, water, or rest. Their chains insured that their info packets would be delivered together, forming the chat rooms and streaming video clips that humans had grown to love.

Olla held out her hand and a giant horsefly landed on her palm. She lightly petted its winged back as an evil plan formed in her mind. Spiders, she would send out spiders. She would release her mutant spiders to track the rebel and capture him in a paralyzing web. It was perfect! Olla let out a laugh and clapped her hands together in delight. Unfortunately for the horsefly, he was not fast enough and was smushed to a wet blob on Olla's hand. When Olla realized that she had flattened the poor horsefly, she happily slurped the gooey mess off her hand.

Olla's mutant spiders were no ordinary spiders. In the Internet, spiders power what humans call search engines. Search engines have spiders that crawl the Internet gathering and indexing information from websites. Olla's mutant spiders had been given extra intelligence to locate specific e-people. Olla had created mutant spiders that searched the Internet looking for the prey she requested. Unlike normal spiders, they attacked their prey when they found it, spinning an inescapable web around it and then returning to Olla to report the prey's location. Olla's mutant spiders never returned without their prey. They would search the Internet forever if they had to.

Pleased with herself, Olla got out of her swampy tub to go see the King and fill him in on her mutant spider plan. She quickly threw back on her dirty robes and padded down the hall toward the king's Control Room, leaving giant wet footsteps behind her.

Olla had a long wait outside of his room before the king agreed to see her and hear her plan. "Well, go ahead. What have you devised?" the king asked impatiently.

"I'm going to send out two of my black mutant spiders to track and find him. I'll send one out searching for "rebel" and one searching for "e-boy," Olla said with a huge smile on her face, extremely pleased with her brilliant plan.

Henry sat silently, while his face quickly turned from a pale pink to bright pink to fuming purple. Grasping the handles of his throne so tightly his knuckles whitened, he spat between clenched teeth. "How many times do I have to explain to you how your stupid spiders work! You can't do a search for 'e-boy' or you'll get all 711,752 e-boys. Do you think I want *every* e-boy cocooned in a web here in the castle? You're as dumb as my brother!"

Nearby, Sebastian pretended to be in a fit of coughing to cover up his uncontrollable laughter.

"Well I, um, oh I, humph, I guess, um..." Olla tried to come up with an answer to please the king but her slug-slow brain left her without a clue.

Annoyed with the stupidity of his right-hand woman, Henry pounded his fist on a nearby table, which called up his Omnipotent 5000. This super-computer kept photos and information and tracked the work of *every* e-person and router in the Land of the Internet. While Olla had been soaking in her swamp, Henry had looked through the deliveries of the Stealth Carrier e-boys to find out whose had not been completed in the last few days. Although it was clear that someone was delivering some of the packets, an e-boy named E-Wally was obviously the runaway. With a few quick and angry key stokes, Henry printed E-Wally's information and photo.

"While you were dreaming up your really smart plan," Henry said in a mocking voice, "I found out who he is. His name is E-Wally." Henry threw the paper at Olla's feet. "Now do a search that will work. Do a search for *E-Wally* and your disgusting spiders will actually find who we are looking for."

Henry rose from his chair to leave; he had had

enough of Olla for one day. Olla picked up the paper with E-Wally's name and picture. Turning, she lumbered back to the Cavern.

Olla went to the darkest and farthest corner of the Cavern and reached her arm through a web-covered alcove. Ripping through the webs she pulled out one mutant spider. "Ahhh, you beauty," she muttered, tucking it securely into the pocket of her robes. Plowing her thick arm through the web a second time, she caught another hairy mutant. She carried the two spiders back to her long, marble worktable.

Pinning the first spider down with her left hand, she firmly took her tattooing needle with her right hand. Hot orange current flowed from the needle, burning the short hairs on the spider's back leaving a blazing orange trail behind. She looked proudly at the word *E-Wally* inscribed on the spider's back. Reaching for a clear glass dome from a nearby shelf, Olla carefully placed it over the dazed mutant spider.

Olla reached deep into her musky pocket and grabbed the second spider. This was the more difficult task. The image she'd tattoo on this spider's back had to be perfect. Olla concentrated with all her might. The effort was so great that soon her broad forehead was drenched in sweat, but the result was worth the pain. Henry would love her for the incredible job she'd done. At long last the spiders were ready to be released the following morning.

She knew the spiders would not rest until they had trapped E-Wally in a web and returned with the location of the entrapped e-boy. She had purposely made their tattoos different so that no website or line would be left unvisited. One mutant spider would look for the word *E-Wally* as a clue to his location and the other would search for the e-boy's face in case he was surfing the lines between websites. Olla yawned and headed for bed. Nestling cozily under covers she snuggled deep into her nest of bug wings and empty cocoons. She would have a wonderful nap. Her plan was foolproof.

CHAPTER SIX

STEVEN'S PLAN

At that time E-Wally was sitting on the edge of his slide and holding his head in his hands. He closed his eyes and pictured his family — his mom's warm face, his silly little brother who always made him laugh, and, of course, his wise and loving grandfather. There was no question. "I'm going back," pledged E-Wally to himself.

Just then Justin burst in from school, "Hi, E-Wally! Things went so great today at school. I got to tell the whole class about what I had learned about T and his family. Now my friend Steven wants to teach a class of his own and...guess what! Miss Restrepo said he could," he typed happily.

"That's good," E-Wally answered, trying to smile. Justin was really proud. "I mean it's great, really great," he added, trying to look happy. Justin wasn't fooled. He could tell that something was wrong with E-Wally.

"What's wrong?" Justin typed carefully.

"Well, I've been thinking about my grandpa. I'm never gonna be able to help him if I stay here. I've gotta go back home." E-Wally didn't mention the butterflies that fluttered in his stomach at the thought of heading home. He didn't want to worry his friend. "I want to go get my grandpa. Can I bring him back here to your hard drive with me?"

"Sure you can bring your grandpa back here. But do you think it's safe? What if you have to battle another router?"

The two boys talked all through the night and by morning it was decided. E-Wally was going home.

"Before you go I have to do one thing," said Justin. He quickly went online to www.Ronjons.com to download one last thing for his friend. In a moment he was back with a "No Fear" baseball cap. "For good luck, to make up for the one that creepy fuzzball stole off you."

E-Wally turned his new baseball cap backwards

and squared his jaw into a determined line. He was anticipating a speedy trip. He adjusted his black sunglasses and confidently turned to his friend and waved good-bye.

E-Wally grabbed both sides of his hyper transport board, took a run, and hopped gracefully into a surfer crouch. E-Wally disappeared toward his quest in a brilliant flash of light.

✴

E-Wally's friend Pete was making his second delivery of the day. He was daydreaming more than usual, still amazed at the extraordinary sight of E-Wally battling the fuzzball router the day before. If E-Wally could be a rebel than maybe he and their friend Eddie could too. His daydream was interrupted by a strong stench in the air and that could only mean one thing — Olla Brac. She was hunched over at the side of the line. Curious, Pete slowed up and cautiously edged closer. It looked like she was releasing something. Whatever it was, it couldn't be good.

He peered warily around her bulky robes and saw that she was opening the doors of two black cages. Out from the cages sprang two hairy, long-legged spiders. They scurried down the line right past Pete. As the spiders brushed by him, Pete gasped at the orange tattoos on their backs. One was a clear image of E-Wally's face and the other spider was emblazoned with one word — *E-Wally*.

"Oh no," Pete panicked. "Olla's launched a search for E-Wally. I've gotta warn him." Pete reached into his mailbag and grabbed his digital communicator. Each of the three boys had a communicator, which Eddie had invented last year. They loved to play with them, sending messages during long, hard days at work. Would E-Wally have taken his with him? Pete began trying to reach E-Wally. "E-Wally, E-Wally, come in E-Wally," he repeated urgently. Again and again he tried to send his message through. "Turn on your communicator, E-Wally. Please have it with you. Turn it on." Pete feared that E-Wally was out there with no clue to the terrible fate about to befall him.

Miles away along the backbone of the Internet, E-Wally was slowly surfing along while trying to plan his next move. He was building a strategy that would get him to Grandpa and home by passing through the fewest routers possible. When E-Wally heard the familiar static coming from his digital communicator, he pulled the tiny apparatus from his pocket. The voice was so weak E-Wally could barely hear Pete calling to him, "E-Wally, E-Wally are you there?"

When E-Wally answered, Pete burst in and said,

"I saw you yesterday. Where'd you get that hyper transport board? What crazy idea made you think you could battle a router? Are you okay?"

"Where were you? How'd you see me?"

"I was in the queue. It was amazing. But listen, we can't talk now. I just saw Olla. She released two of her mutant spiders and they're searching for you. Where are you? You've gotta hide off the Internet lines."

His mind raced and his stomach twisted in fear. "I can hide, sure. I've got a place in a hard drive ....but, are you kidding? Mutant spiders?" E-Wally knew Olla's spiders were relentless and searched without rest until they located their prey. "Listen, Pete. I've got to get off this line and back to my friend's hard drive. If they're loose they'll be on me in no time. Go, work, don't cause suspicion... and thanks, thanks a lot, buddy." With that E-Wally was off at breakneck speed, hurtling into Justin's hard drive before the spiders traced him.

Ruthie heard Justin yell, "E-Wally!" *Why was E-Wally back so soon?* She ran to Justin's room and gazed in at the monitor. E-Wally was pale and sweating so much that his spikey hair drooped onto his forehead. Something must have gone horribly wrong. "What happened? Why are you back already?"

It didn't take long for E-Wally to recount Pete's frightening warning. He explained about Olla's mutant spiders. E-Wally hung his head and said, "I had to come back. It was too risky, too scary."

"No," said Justin as E-Wally sat down at the base of the tree. "You did the right thing. Bravery isn't stupidity. Without a plan you'd be in real danger. We've gotta figure out how to beat this thing. We'll do it together."

"You don't understand: I have to bring Grandpa back here before Olla takes him away. She gave him a warning, but it was just for one week. And now I'm in so much trouble, she'll probably take him anyway."

At first Justin couldn't even think — a mutant spider? *What kind of people are King Henry and Olla?* "I don't know what to do. Darn, and I have to go to school right now. Please, E-Wally, just stay here and wait. We'll come up with a plan and you'll be out of here tonight."

Although he was eager to help his grandpa, hanging out all day with Xena sounded perfect to the exhausted and overwhelmed E-Wally. He needed time to think. The kids went off to school while their e-friend took a much needed rest. By the time Justin reached third period, science class, he still had not come up with a plan. "Hey, why so serious?" asked Steven as he slid into his desk right behind Justin's.

Justin looked up at his best friend and wondered if he should tell Steven about E-Wally. No one knew about his e-friend, not even Steven. Steven was the smartest kid he knew. He was also not a big mouth. Justin thought for a moment and decided that Steven could keep a secret. Then the bell rang and Mrs. Restrepo started on a long lecture. "Listen up, class. Open your notebooks and be sure to take notes. You will be tested on this."

Justin whispered, "Meet me at lunch, I have something important to tell you."

"Me too," whispered Steven, "Mrs. Restrepo said that I could do a lesson for the class like you did about dinosaurs. She said I could pick the topic and I'm going to do entomology."

"Entomology, what's that?"

"I'll tell you at lunch."

Two hours later Steven and Justin were sitting in front of trays of mystery meat and limp green beans in the quietest corner of the cafeteria. Steven was excitedly explaining, "I found this website called 'Young Entomologist Society' and it tells all about insects, bugs, and spiders. I put a picture of my tarantula on the site and three kids from a school in Mississippi wrote to me. It's so cool."

"I can't believe you're telling me this, " said Justin, laughing and shaking his head. The rest of lunch flew by. Justin started at the beginning and told Steven everything, including the way E-Wally got to his hard drive by delivering an e-mail from Steven.

At the end of the story Steven said, "Well, let's

go! We've got to get to your house now. We have work to do."

"We can't go now," replied Justin, looking quizzically at his best friend. Steven never skipped school and they had three more hours of class.

"Get Ruthie and I'll go to the library. There's one book I need to get. I'll meet you two at the corner of the gym. Justin, don't wimp out now, this is important!"

Justin didn't wait. Of course they had to go home. E-Wally's life was in danger. Five minutes later all three kids were racing across the school field toward Oak Street. They ran the entire eleven blocks to 297 Pinnacle Drive. With Mom and Dad at work, it was no trouble to race up the stairs and into Justin's room unnoticed.

Click, the mouse click opened the tree house file. Steven breathed a quiet, "Wow."

"E-Wally, remember the e-mail you delivered to me the first night? Remember the J you were hiding behind? That was an e-mail from Steven. He's my best friend. Well, my best human friend, anyway," said Justin as an introduction.

"You won't believe this, E-Wally," Ruthie interrupted, unable to stay quiet a moment longer. "Steven knows all about entomology — spider stuff! He can save you, E-Wally. Like maybe he can copy his gross old tarantula into a video file and let it chase Olla and have her for dinner."

"Is that true? Can you do stuff like that?" questioned E-Wally, full of hope. He ran to the front of the file and leaned against the monitor screen. "How will you copy a tarantula?"

"I can't do that," replied Steven leaning his face in to get a better look at this cool e-boy wearing a "No Fear" baseball cap.

"So how are you going to save E-Wally?" Ruthie asked Steven. She was ready to get on with this. She wanted to send E-Wally on his way. It seemed like she'd been waiting to meet Grandpa forever, and they had to hurry before he was taken by Olla.

"Whoa, wait a minute. I don't even know what kind of spider it is."

"Well, ask him then," insisted Ruthie as she shoved the keyboard at Steven.

Steven cautiously began to type his first message to E-Wally and asked him about the spiders inside the Internet. Ruthie held up the large book Steven had checked out of the library. E-Wally looked closely at pictures of daddy longlegs, tarantulas, and black widows. At the third picture E-Wally jumped up. "That's it, that's what Olla's mutant spiders look like."

E-Wally went on, explaining the role of spiders in his land. They share the lines harmlessly with e-people, crawling from site to site, indexing information. Olla's mutant spiders, which looked like the picture of the black widow, were much more intelligent. Their brains were four times the normal size. They would seek out whatever Olla tattooed on their backs and then spin their prey into a paralyzing cocoon.

"Did you ever see that happen to anyone?" Justin leaned, wide-eyed, closer to the monitor. "What happens to the e-person in the web?"

"It's the most terrible thing I've ever seen. The mutant spiders leave their prey in a sticky web stuck to the ground and go get Olla, who drags them back to her Cavern. Once my e-friend Rayanne tried to help her dad and she stuck to the web. Both of them were dragged off by Olla and we never saw them again."

Justin turned to Steven. "The spiders won't rest until they find E-Wally. We've got to figure out how to kill them."

Steven sat quietly for a minute. *What kills spiders?* Then it hit him. "The biggest enemy for insects are other animals. They eat each other all the time," he said. At that Xena hopped up and down. She was hoping no other animals would visit her file. There was no way she wanted to share bugs with anyone or anything.

"Don't you guys remember that scary movie we saw, *Arachnophobia*?" Ruthie said. She shuddered, remembering the attack of thousands of spiders. "Come on, let's think!"

They were all quiet, frowning in concentration.

Ruthie twisted a curl of her hair and Justin bit his fingernails. E-Wally could almost see thoughts whirring in their heads. Suddenly, at the same moment, Justin and Steven jumped up shouting, "I've got it!" It took the two boys just minutes to explain their plans. Justin's used all of his computer knowledge and Steven's made use of his obsessive love of bugs. Like lawyers in a courtroom anxiously awaiting the decision of the jury, both boys stared expectantly at E-Wally. Which solution would E-Wally select? It was a no-brainer, E-Wally grinned from ear to ear. His decision flashed onto the screen: "You guys are awesome. We'll do them both." In Justin's room and in the tree house file, the group jubilantly shouted, hugged, and danced.

Since Steven needed help on the computer to make his plan work, Ruthie volunteered to help him in her room. Justin and E-Wally got to work on his plan. "Your plan will create the perfect trap, the sorry mutant will be scuttling into it in no time. This plan is gonna work," E-Wally said, with fingers crossed for good luck. "It just better work."

The two boys got to work. Knowing that the spiders search websites, Justin's plan was to build a web page about E-Wally linked to his school's website. Justin had recently been voted school webmaster and given the passwords to update the website. "I should be able to figure out how to make a website that can fool the stupid mutants. We'll lure Olla's spiders to a web page somehow. We'll make them think they found you when it's really just a trap."

Both boys knew this was life and death. If their plans didn't work, E-Wally would be defenseless against Olla Brac. Justin's hands were clammy, but he began typing. Justin created a web page with bright blue letters that said, "E-Wally is here. Come and get me, Olla." To entice the spiders even more, they decided to include a graphic called ewally.jpg. E-Wally had posed for the image by standing tall. He put a finger in each corner of his mouth, pulled it wide and shouted, "Naaah, naaaah, naaaaah," making an angry face. It was easy. He just imagined what he wished he could do if he saw Olla. Justin added text to the graphic, so across E-Wally's chest it read, "Come and get me, Olla." Justin inserted the graphic into the page.

Reading on in his computer book, Justin learned that spiders look for meta tags. "The spiders will be looking for meta tags about you," he typed to E-Wally. The book said that meta tags are words, descriptions, and phrases that are written in HTML. As the school webmaster, Justin knew all about HTML. It was a language just like French or English. It was a simple programming language for web pages.

The two boys would have to think of lots of descriptions of E-Wally to lure the mutant spiders to their site. Once the spiders found the site, they would think they had found E-Wally and bring Olla to the site. That would give E-Wally enough time to get Grandpa and bring him back to Justin's hard drive.

Justin closed E-Wally's tree house file. He opened the file for E-Wally's web page and created the meta tags. Steven and Ruthie walked into the room as Justin was uploading the page. "I wonder if it's okay for me to be putting this on the school server. I never used it for anything but school web pages before."

"Oh, man, don't be stupid. You've got to save E-Wally and his family. It's mutant spiders we're luring here. This is no hacking or game we're playing. This is serious, Justin," said Steven, dismissing Justin's worries. They clicked open the file where E-Wally had been waiting expectantly.

"Is it done?" breathed E-Wally, jumping from where he had been sitting, wired and worried.

"Done, and it's good!" gleamed Steven.

Ruthie couldn't contain herself a moment longer. "Can I give it to him now, Steven?" she asked proudly, holding out a yellow diskette.

"It's now or never. Sure, load it up and copy the secret weapon for E-Wally. Hopefully you won't need it," said Steven confidently.

Ruthie looked expectantly at E-Wally, then her smile vanished. "Wait!" shrieked Ruthie, grabbing the keyboard from Steven. " We've got your plans for getting past the spiders, but how are you going to get past the fuzzball routers with that wild shirt and your hyper transport board? You can't fight *every* one of them all the way home."

A leaden silence fell on the trio. "Go put on your uniform, E-Wally. Hurry. I have an idea, I'll be right back." Ruthie flew from the room and the boys could hear her click-click-clicking away on her keyboard. Knowing what a little artist his sister was, Justin figured she was making a graphic of some kind. They didn't have to wonder long. By the time E-Wally climbed down from the tree house in his faded old uniform, Ruthie was back with a green diskette. "Here, try this." She loaded the graphic into E-Wally's file.

A dull, clunky, and slow-looking transport board appeared next to the royal blue hyper transport board. With a quick cut and paste Ruthie had covered E-Wally's hyper transport board. "There, the old fuzzballs will have a harder time spotting you. But do you think it will maneuver just as good as ever?"

"I think so. I mean you just covered it up. His good board is still there and not changed a single bit. Now go, go, E-Wally," said Steven, starting to really feel tense. Urgency electrified the air.

"Come on," begged Justin, barely able to control his nerves, "Those spiders could already be hung up in the page so you better get going if you're going to sneak past the nasty little demons."

The inevitable departure could be delayed no longer. "I'm off," he yelled and with that, E-Wally burst from the safety of the hard drive for what could be his last time. All thoughts were on home, his family, and, especially, Grandpa.

✳

CHAPTER SEVEN

ATTACK OF THE MUTANT SPIDER

No sooner was E-Wally past the server when he saw what he was most dreading: one of Olla's giant mutants. Eight hairy, jointed legs clattering in rapid succession carried the giant spider directly toward him. Its front legs were outstretched, rocking up and down with each frantic step the spider took. The spider was now so close that E-Wally could see his own name emblazoned on the bulbous black body. Its flaming red eyes seemed focused directly at E-Wally's face. Momentarily he froze in fear. *This is it.*

Then, as if startled, the spider bolted in the opposite direction. For the moment the coast was clear and there was no other spider in sight. E-Wally couldn't believe his good fortune. *Is it good fortune? Will the spider come back?* E-Wally couldn't think of that right now, since he had five routers to pass. That would be a challenge for sure, but he was up to it. He was on his way home.

Some brand of luck would have it that all the queues were hectic and the fuzzball routers were deliriously checking off e-people. They were frazzled and half blinded by their rat's nests of hair and less attentive than usual to the frantic e-crowds trying to complete their assignment quotas. The first three routers had unusually thick crowds. Three times E-Wally managed to blend in with the queues, and he could barely believe his luck. In spite of what seemed like good fortune, he never relaxed or let down his guard for a moment. Every movement to the right or the left of him sent a shiver down his spine, but so far none had been a mutant.

✦

Back in Olla's Cavern, Olla was pampering the spider tattooed with E-Wally's name. Feeding it the most juicy and delectable fly in her collection, she learned that the spider had located the runaway e-boy. She was barely able to control her excitement as the spider polished off the fly. Olla imagined how grateful King Henry would be. In a very short time when she deposited a well-cocooned captured e-boy, he might even embrace her in glee. They'd probably dine together in his private banquet room, toasting their success. Her daydream abruptly ended as the last bit of fly wing disappeared with a final slurp into the mutant's mouth.

Olla used the spider as her guide to the website. Her lumbering bulk slowed down the trip immensely, but the spider could be patient. Once Olla returned with the object defined in her search, the spider anticipated a few more savory flies. Focused on following the spider, a panting, sweating, happy Olla plodded along on her favorite sort of mission.

At last E-Wally reached the fourth router. He tested the air for a hint of Olla. No stench, but still he had to hurry. E-Wally worried about getting past this router. The crowds had thinned now, as this was a less traveled route. Whether this was good fortune or not, the next moments would tell. E-Wally cruised up to the line and studied the bowed hairy head of a rather slow-moving fuzzball. This guy looked like a sleepy sort. He was barely paying attention as e-deliverers passed by. E-Wally was fourth in line at the queue and the fuzzball was drowsily, almost robotically, checking off each e-person. Barely looking at them, the fuzzball haphazardly glanced up and down the line as each new arrival surfed in to place. E-Wally had a feeling he'd be able to slip right past this router. Mere seconds later, he had! No spiders appeared, the line looked clear, and he had just one more before home.

Shadows deepened along the Internet lines, and an almost foreboding atmosphere crept in with the encroaching gloom. Although this was the most familiar part of the lines for E-Wally, so close to home, today the atmosphere was different. He wondered if the mutants were near. No time to think about that; E-Wally realized his problems were just beginning. "Oh no," he muttered under his breath. Just two people ahead of him was his mom's best friend, Large Marge. "Uck," he said to himself. He had enough to worry about with spiders and fuzzball routers. Marge made a career out of heckling E-Wally and his little brother, Maxter.

"Be quiet. Finish your work. Get another packet," was all she ever said. She never tired of torturing them. How would he ever explain where he had been, and what else would she want to know? When she abruptly turned, E-Wally tried to duck behind his board so she wouldn't see him at all. Too late.

"E-Wally, is that you?" she bellowed in her nasal-

ATTACK OF THE MUTANT SPIDER

ly voice. "I saw you. You'd better not be hiding. Don't
think you can hide!"

He hid his head behind his board, "Aw, bugs." He
felt his face turn as red as the tropical flowers on his
shirt. Now everyone in line would be looking at him.
Large Marge was relentless. This was no time to have
attention drawn his way. The spider could be honing
in on him from any direction at any moment.

"You come out from behind that board, boy. I
don't know where you've been hiding. Your mother's
been heartsick. We've been looking all over for you.
Your brother Maxter's been crying himself to sleep
every night. So just come out from behind that board,
boy!" Marge's voice cracked like a whip, urging E-
Wally to heed her demand.

E-Wally kicked at the ground. There was no hiding, and E-Wally came from behind his board. "Hello,
Miss Marge," he said meekly. His eyes darted in
every direction, keeping a keen lookout for the mutants. He waited for the onslaught of words he knew
would be coming.

"My word, what are you wearing under your uniform? And what on earth sort of transport board do
you have? Where have you been?" Hardly pausing or
waiting for an answer she ranted on. E-Wally wondered how she could go on and on without ever taking a breath. Before he had a chance to even think
of an answer, Large Marge was interrupted by the out-

raged cries of e-people behind them being cut out of the router queue.

When E-Wally swung around to see the outraged e-people leaving the queue, his breath caught sharply. "Grandpa!" E-Wally shouted in a voice full of frustration, fear, and a sadness so huge it threatened to choke him. His words were strangled in his throat. The sight of Grandpa, balanced precariously on his rickety old board, started Large Marge up on one more rant.

"See what you've done to your grandfather. You selfish boy, none of your family has slept in days. They've been trying to deliver your packets with theirs so that no one would notice you were gone. You're just as bad as your uncle Anzwar, running off to do your own thing! This is the fourth time E-Liam has been turned away from this queue today. He's working himself to death."

Thankfully Marge finally reached the front of the queue. The router let her through, sending her on her way. He had to do something. There was no way E-Wally could let Grandpa be turned away from the queue again. Unfortunately, E-Wally didn't have time to think of a way to save his grandpa. He'd been so distracted by Large Marge's ranting and worried about how tired and weak his grandpa looked, he had momentarily forgotten all about Olla's spiders.

E-Wally felt a sharp pain in the back of his neck

like a needle driving into his spine. "Ahhhh!" he screamed first in shock and then in pain as two more agonizing needle-sharp pinchers drove into his shoulders. He couldn't keep his balance. He was being forced face first into the ground. The pain sounded an alarm in E-Wally's head: *Spiders!* He was being attacked! Over his own screams, he heard the collective panic of the e-people around him. They were trying to hurry past the spider and get out of the router queue as fast as possible. The fuzzball router was so interested in the spider that e-people poured by him two at a time.

As E-Liam entered the router queue, three of his friends turned and blocked his path. "What's going on fellows?" he asked, worried about the screaming and commotion he heard in front of him.

His friends quickly looked at one another, not wanting to be the one who'd break the terrible news that Olla's spider had gotten E-Wally. It took only that brief hesitation for wise E-Liam to recognize the screams as those of his eldest grandson. "E-Wally! Is it E-Wally?" he yelled, trying to force his way past his old friends.

"Stop, E-Liam, it's too late! One of Olla's mutant spiders has him." The friends held E-Liam back.

"Let me pass! Let go of me." E-Liam thrashed and pushed with all his might.

"No! You can't help. If you try, it'll take you too!"

They all knew that E-Wally's rebellious actions of the last few days were going to end in a horrible way. It was the way of King Henry's rule. There was no use in E-Liam's being taken too. His poor daughter would be heartsick to hear her eldest son had been taken. After all she had already lost, it would kill her to lose her father in the same day.

With strength they had not known they had for years, the three men picked up E-Liam and dragged him past the router, the spider, and E-Wally. They dragged him all the way out of the router queue. As he passed, E-Liam let out a strangled cry, "E-Wally," choking back the tears.

The sight was horrible indeed. The spider had pinned E-Wally down, face first onto the ground. The disgusting mutant stood on E-Wally's back with his hairy legs pinning the boy down. Each of the monster's legs ended in a thin, sharp point. These pierced through E-Wally's uniform, pricking his back with eight razor-sharp cuts. E-Wally squirmed and wiggled in panic, trying to get the disgusting creature off of him. With each move the razorlike feet of the spider cut him more. He stopped for a minute, trying to slow down his racing mind. The pressure of the spider's leg on his back made it hard for him to breathe. He struggled for one deep breath. He smelled the pungent odor of burnt hair. The spider was beginning to weave its web.

The spider turned and started with the rebel e-boy's legs. They were kicking and flailing and bothering him. It would be best to tie them down first. The spider worked quickly, spinning out hot, sticky webbing across E-Wally's feet and legs.

"No! Urgg!" E-Wally hollered, trying to kick off the sticky webbing. He knew he didn't have much time. Soon the webbing would be so thick he would be powerless. His kicking just made the situation worse. Every time he lifted his leg to kick, the webbing stuck to the front of his ankle and foot so that when he lowered his leg it stuck even more firmly to the ground. He struggled to get one of his hands free, but the gigantic spider had firmly pinned down each of E-Wally's arms at the wrist.

The spider was working quickly. E-Wally's feet were so heavy with webbing that he could no longer move them. His ankles were now stuck together as the spider scooted up toward E-Wally's head and got to work on the top of his legs.

"Ack, get off me you mutant freak!" E-Wally hollered as he tried to control his coughing and gagging. The fumes from the mutant's fresh, hot webbing were overpowering and coated his nose, burning his chest as he breathed.

Realizing that he was not going to be able to free either of his hands, E-Wally thought of a new plan. He didn't have half a second to spare as the spider crept closer to his head. He turned his face to the side and started to flip his head wildly back and forth. It didn't work. He tried again, this time shaking his head fiercely from side to side. It still didn't work.

The disgusting beast was starting to get annoyed with the feisty e-boy's head shaking. That's when E-Wally's luck changed. The spider scooted up toward E-Wally's head so it could sit on it while it webbed his arms and torso. The gigantic mutant's aim was not as good as he thought it was. As he struggled to get the e-boy's head under his butt, he knocked E-Wally's hat right off.

The hat rolled to the ground and in a brilliant white blaze of light Steven and Ruthie's secret weapon appeared. The spider froze in fear at the sight before him. Ruthie and Steven had written an animated graphic of an enormous and very hungry frog. Once released from under E-Wally's cap, the frog inflated to gigantic proportions, compliments of a perfectly written animation "enlarge" command. The program caused the frog to increase to forty times its normal size. The spider cowered beneath the shadow of the monstrous frog. E-Wally propped himself up on his elbows in awe at his now-monumental frog. The spider's red beady eyes bulged in terror as its fate became clear. In one sweeping motion, the frog opened its gargantuan mouth and its tongue sprang out. As if directed by radar, the tongue unfurled towards the mutant spider. With the speed of lightening, it snatched the spider and sucked it back into its mouth. E-Wally watched in disbelief at the sight of the spider rolled up in the frog's tongue.

Ready to jump for joy, E-Wally tried to stand up. The spider had weaved the web tightly, and E-Wally was no match for it. The frog must have still been hungry for more, because it began to gently lick the warm webbing off of E-Wally's legs. Within seconds he was free. Steven's trick had worked. E-Wally's voice exploded in relief, "Hold on Grandpa, I'm coming home!"

Fiber optic lines ahead took E-Wally along at breakneck speed and he breathed his first sigh of relief. The energy that had pulsed so strongly through his veins faded, leaving him feeling worn out. Soon the line E-Wally was traveling on intersected with the main line nearest to his home. Gratefully E-Wally surfed onto it.

Eddie and Pete spotted E-Wally from a distant queue. Waving excitedly, they surfed to his side eager to hear what had happened since they last talked. They were absolutely amazed to see E-Wally alive. There were e-people all around staring and pointing at E-Wally.

It was great seeing Eddie and Pete again, but all E-Wally wanted to do at that moment was get home to see Grandpa and his family. Realizing that Pete didn't know the value of his warning him, E-Wally said, "Pete, you saved my life, man. If I hadn't known about the spiders I would've been a goner."

Before Pete could reply, Eddie interrupted. "What's that gunk all over you?" He stuck a finger tentatively on the leftover web wrapped around E-Wally's leg, "Phew, it stinks. What is that stuff?" A look of comprehension spread across both their faces at the same time.

"You battled a mutant spider?" they gasped. "But no one beats the mutants."

"You really beat the spider?" Pete asked. He was already amazed that E-Wally could beat a router, but a spider was another thing altogether.

E-Wally nodded.

"You're kidding me, how?"

Pete wanted every detail. E-Wally and his friends surfed over to a quiet line while he quickly told them about the plans that Justin, Ruthie, and Steven had made for him. He shared each terrifying moment of the spider attack, down to the frog's life-saving swallow.

Knowing they had been part of such an incredible tale, Pete and Eddie felt like powerful conspirators. They were so proud of their friend that they didn't give a thought to Olla's inevitable revenge. Pete hopped on the back of E-Wally's board and grabbed onto his shoulders. E-Wally spun 360 degrees in glee, as the three boys belted out the router song at the top of their lungs.

They entered the street where their families had lived since the beginning of King Henry's reign. The street of metallic houses was quickly filling with E-Wally's neighbors. Some came out to see what all the ruckus was about and others who had heard about the battle with the mutant spider came out to see if E-Wally had survived. Eddie's father, a lean and tall e-man, raced from the crowd and scooped up Eddie along with his big old board. "Stop that now, son, come away from that rebel," he ordered.

Shocked, E-Wally froze as Eddie was whipped away and hauled brusquely toward home. Pete's Aunt Gladys strode forward pushing her scrawny body through the mass of onlookers. She grabbed Pete at the scruff of the neck more roughly than one would expect from such a wiry, little thing. "Get off that board. It's not his; it's probably stolen," she barked.

Pete gave E-Wally a quick, confused look before he was rattled down the street as fast as Gladys could drag him.

A deep husky voice shouted from the crowd, " I always knew he'd become a renegade like his Uncle Anzwar."

"Yeah," responded a woman shrilly, "King Henry will find out about this. You think he makes us work hard now, just wait."

Each word was a dart, shooting through E-Wally's spirit. He had expected to battle the router, the spiders, and Olla — but not his neighbors. He just assumed that he was doing the right thing. Why was everyone so angry? He just wanted to go home now, as quickly as he could. Alone, with hunched shoulders under his wild, flowered shirt the little e-boy cruised at top speed over the last, short, lonely distance toward home.

✳

CHAPTER EIGHT

HOMECOMING

E-Wally brought his hyper transport board to an abrupt halt just outside his home. Under the glow from the many wires and routes, the gun-metal surfaces of his domed house gleamed a burnt yellow. Nestled at the corner of two main lines, E-Wally's home may have looked identical to every other home in the Land of the Internet to most, but to E-Wally, it was the most beautiful sight he could imagine. Looking in the window, he could see his horrified family listening to E-Liam describing the terrible sight of E-

Wally's captured by Olla's mutant spider. The young adventurer was suddenly just a homesick little e-boy. E-Wally raced through the door, and his mom, brother, and grandfather leaped from the table, smothering him with hugs.

"E-Wally, you're back. You're safe," they exclaimed.

Then in the same breath his mom cried, "What were you thinking running away like that?" Her large dark eyes filled with tears.

This was not like mom at all. Mom never cried, not even when her brother Anzwar left years ago when E-Wally was a baby, or after Dad disappeared. She stood back, gathering her emotions as best she could while crossing her strong, tan arms and shaking her long, brown braids rapidly. Her sensible half was very angry with her son for the foolish way he had run off, for risking his life. Her other half was proud because he was so much like her beloved older brother, Anzwar.

In frustration and relief, she grabbed her naughty e-boy and gave him the shaking of his lifetime. She couldn't help herself. It was no joke being an e-person under the rule of King Henry. Anzwar was already gone, to who knew where, and no one was sure if Dad would ever return. While E-Wally's brain rattled crazily inside his head, Mom sternly barked, "Don't you ever think of leaving here again. We thought you were dead." His mom impressed upon E-Wally the grave situation that they now faced.

With her hands firmly on her son's shoulders, she glanced up at her father, E-Liam. Their eyes met. A line had been crossed: E-Wally's situation was very grave. After E-Liam had come home earlier that day, pale and devastated, certain his grandson had been captured and sent to Olla, neither had expected to see E-Wally alive again. Now that he was here, now that he had run away and battled both a router and a spider, both adults realized life in their home would never be the same. E-Wally's mom looked sternly into her son's eyes and admonished him with one final warning: "You must stay on your assigned tasks, keep your head down, and mix in with the crowd or Olla will manage to nab you away from us for good."

"Yeah E-Wally," piped up his little brother. As long as E-Wally was safe, he was very excited about the mutant spider attack. Five-year-old Maxter went on. "The kids at school said that Olla Brac found you playing when you should have been working. I said that was a lie, you always work hard, but everyone figured she crushed you or sent a bug out to drag you away. Gross! Disgusting!" gagging, Maxter pretended that just the sound of Olla's name made him very sick.

E-Wally shot Maxter a grin and tossed him on his back for a ride, "No way, I'm fine." But E-Wally could see from the expression on Grandpa's face how serious things really were. E-Wally was still shaken up by remembering the look on Eddie's father's face when he snatched Eddie away from E-Wally. He had acted like E-Wally was a criminal, or, worse, infected with a virus.

"Here you go, Maxter." E-Wally lifted Maxter up and over his head onto the brushed metal chair. E-Wally walked slowly to E-Liam who stood with one hand resting on the warm metallic wall of the kitchen.

"Grandpa, I've been to the websites. I've got human friends, Justin and Ruthie, and a tree house that's way past the server in a hard drive. Justin downloaded me a hyper transport board." Taking his grandpa's hand, E-Wally continued. "I want you to come back with me where Olla can never get you. You wouldn't have to work back at the hard drive, and it's safe there. Please come with me, Grandpa."

This scene was familiar to E-Liam. When his own son, Anzwar, came to him with a similar plea, just before he left to start the rebel forces somewhere in a distant outpost, he had said the same thing. E-Wally couldn't stop the torrent of words. "You won't have to work anymore. You can just rest and be happy." E-Wally stepped close to Grandpa holding his breath and waited for a sign that Grandpa would come with him.

"There'll be time enough for us to talk about this later. Let's finish dinner while it's still hot," said E-Liam as he looked E-Wally square in the eye.

The discussion was over, and suddenly E-Wally was just a hungry young boy, happy to be home for dinner. With a scrambling of chairs and feet the whole family gathered in the warm light of the gray metal kitchen. They ate their dinner of thin potato soup and Bread-Bytes. After dinner they all gave their attention to E-Wally as he told the tales of Justin, Ruthie, T-Rex, Theo, and the websites. Grandpa smiled. The family had a new storyteller in their midst. Later, everyone had a turn at standing on the hyper transport board. Maxter tried on the strange and wonderful flowered shirt and bright, baggy shorts E-Wally wore now in place of the drab postman uniform they were all so used to. Soon, the moon rose full and it was time for sleep. The kids were exhausted — too tired to resist as Mom and E-Liam tucked them into bed. Nothing had ever felt so delicious to E-Wally as the warmth of his own digitized comforter. He looked over at little Maxter snuggled cozily with his blanket in his nearby bed. " 'Night, Maxter."

" 'Night, E-Wally." Maxter was happy to have his brother nearby.

E-Liam and Eleanor had just sat down at the kitchen table to talk when a knock rapped at the door. Eleanor stood up and crossed the small room in two steps to answer the door before the insistent rapping woke up the boys. "Who is it?" she whispered, fearing who this late night visitor might be.

"Eleanor, it's me, Marge. Open up."

E-Wally's mom opened the door and stepped outside, relieved to greet her friend.

"Marge, what are you doing here so late?"

Shifting her hefty weight from side to side, Marge began, "We have to talk. What are you going to do with E-Wally? You must make him leave. You can't have a renegade, a rebel, living in your home."

"You're wrong, Marge," Eleanor interrupted, putting up her hand as if to deflect her friend's ugly accusations. "He's not a renegade; he's just a boy!"

"He may be just a boy in age, but not in his actions," said Marge pointedly with a wag of her thick index finger. "You know that King Henry is sure to find out about his fight with the router and the way he killed Olla's mutant spider. He's gone too far with his wild clothes and that fast board he has no right to use. Rumors of a runaway e-boy have been spread far and wide across the Land of the Internet. We all realized it had to be E-Wally. No one else's son was missing and no one else's son had run off like an irresponsible brat. King Henry has obviously sent Olla Brac on a mission to locate E-Wally."

A chill raced down Eleanor's spine at the mention of Olla Brac. Eleanor had lost too many friends and family members to Olla's wrath over the years, all for crimes infinitely smaller than E-Wally's recent rebellious acts.

Marge continued with her lecture. "Eleanor, really, you must make a decision. You must do something. If Olla catches him she'll turn him over to Henry who's sure to throw him into a relay gang, if not a streaming gang. That is, if he doesn't kill the boy."

"Marge!" Eleanor cried out in disbelief that her closest friend would even think such a thing. "I have to go, Marge. I have to go." E-Wally's mom quickly stepped back into the house and shut the door before Marge could say anything more. Shrugging and shaking her head, Marge headed home, full of more rumors to spread.

Eleanor leaned her back against the door and held her hand to her heart as if to keep it from leaping out of her chest. *The relay gang, the streaming video gang! How could Marge even suggest such things.* Yet she knew it was true. She simply could not imagine such a horrible fate for her beloved E-Wally. She imagined her son with the poor e-people in the streaming gangs, racing from one computer to another carrying immensely heavy packets of video and audio.

Eleanor shook her head vigorously to get the image out of her head. "Not my E-Wally," she said out loud. With a determined breath she added, "Not my E-Wally. I won't allow it."

"Neighbors?" E-Liam asked as he hobbled over to the front door to speak with his daughter.

"Marge," Eleanor answered stepping closer to her dad.

"Ha, I should have guessed that now, shouldn't I. I'm sure she gave you an ear full."

"Oh, Dad, what'll we do? He's just a boy. Does he even understand what he's done? I fear Olla Brac will certainly come for him."

E-Liam reached out his wrinkled, knotted hand and firmly held his strong daughter's shoulder. "He knows. He knows what he's done. He may be your little boy, but he's a child no longer. Pete saw him battle the router. From the sounds of the clash, he rides that board better than any I have ever seen. Made me a bit jealous not to be able to ride against a fuzzball myself, I have to admit," E-Liam explained with a smile dancing in his eyes. "Can you even fathom the will and determination it took for him to come back home knowing spiders were after him? Eleanor, he battled a spider and won. Have you ever heard of anyone doing that? He's strong and brave, with a loving heart driving his actions."

Reaching a hand to touch her father's weathered cheek, Eleanor interrupted, "I know he's brave and good, Dad. He's your grandson after all."

But E-Liam's steady voice continued as he looked straight into Eleanor's eyes. "There's more to it. There is something you haven't realized yet. He can never go back to being your little boy. Independence is in his soul now. He will never go back to fitting in the crowd like you told him earlier. He'll never go back to delivering packets – even if Henry and Olla were to let him go free in spite of his disobedience ..."

"Which we know they won't," she finished the sentence for him.

"No, they won't."

"What should we do? I can't let him be sent to a streaming gang or put into the hands of Olla. I just won't allow it. I can't," Eleanor declared.

"No, we can't let that happen. The boy wants to return to his friend's hard drive and he wants me to go with him. Now you and I both know that I'm slowing down every day. I won't be able to keep up with my quotas for long. When I can't, the foul stench of Olla will visit this house with more than a warning."

E-Liam put each of his gnarled hands firmly on Eleanor's shoulders and looked her straight in the eyes. "Now, I want my grandson to know his history, to know where he came from. I want to teach him so that he will carry himself with pride. I think fate holds a great position for that boy of ours. Before he battles to change the future he must understand his past."

Eleanor sat down, suddenly exhausted under the weight of what she was hearing. "What are you saying, Dad?"

"Ever since he ran from home those few days ago your boy has been a hero. A hero's bravery does not strike a person like a mood, coming and going like a change in the weather. It is born in one's spirit and if it is born there, that is fate. Fate means he has a destiny to fulfill."

Eleanor was silent. Her head and heart ached for the loss she was about to bear. She had lost so many people in her thirty short years. Her heart had been sick without E-Wally for the past few days and now she would lose not only her beloved son, but her father too. She knew there was no other solution.

Eleanor had been told the legend since she was a little girl. Before her death Queen Cyberlina, Henry's mother, had prophesied that a hero would come. The hero would be a new leader for the e-people. The hero would defeat King Henry and lead the e-people out from under his miserable reign. When Anzwar had first left, rebellious and determined, the e-people believed he would find a way to rid the land of King Henry. E-Liam had not spoken of fate or heroes or destiny then. Now looking into her father's eyes she knew that behind all of his words of bravery, fate, and destiny what he was really saying, praying for, was that E-Wally was to be that hero. Her own son might just be the one destined to save the e-people.

"If he can save you, if he can get you to a safe place then I want you to go. Olla's getting closer to stealing you from us every day. I couldn't bear that. Dad, go get E-Wally and go now. Go now while there is less traffic, and the lines are dark and the routers are drowsy. Go before Olla realizes what E-Wally's done. You'll need every possible advantage to make the trip safely."

Knowing that the time was right E-Liam climbed the stairs to go and wake E-Wally. "E-Wally, if we're going, we have to go now."

Mom was standing just behind Grandpa. E-Wally caught her eye and gave her a questioning look. He wondered if she was okay with this. E-Wally quickly threw off his pajamas and dressed in his surfer clothes. Before he joined Grandpa and Mom in the kitchen, he wrote a note to Maxter. He promised to come back as soon as he could.

*

Grandpa held tight to E-Wally on the back of the hyper transport board as his beard streamed behind him in the cyber breeze. The unlikely duo cut this way and that using a back-line path toward Justin's computer. E-Wally maneuvered through the wires like a pro. E-Liam balanced, holding tight to E-Wally's red flowered shirt-tails, shadowing the boy's bold maneuvers. *This boy is destined for greatness,* he thought while cyber wind whistled past his ears. They sped into the server closest to Justin's house and were soon skimming down into Justin's hard drive.

Meanwhile, all through that fateful night in many of the bedrooms throughout E-Wally's neighborhood, there was a whispering between husbands and wives behind closed doors and under the cloak of darkened rooms.

"Could he be the one?"

"He is just a child."

"But he is E-Liam's grandson," they whispered and wondered.

✳

CHAPTER NINE

THE QUEST

Now Grandpa had been many places and had seen many things, but he had never imagined anything like what he found in Justin's hard drive. Soft green leaves blew in the breeze, and the red canvas roof tucked among the branches topped the most incredible house Grandpa had ever seen. There was a rope ladder nearby, and a worn hemp rope beckoned them both to swing on up to the low hanging branches.

"Go on Grandpa," urged E-Wally, taking the hemp rope and handing it to E-Liam. Grandpa grabbed the rope, took a few steps backward, and then with a quick jump began to swing from the rope. "That's it Grandpa. Try again, and this time really push off so you can swing up toward the first branches."

On the second try, Grandpa ran back and gave a loud, "Wheeeeee," as he leaped higher while pulling up with rickety old arms. Like a kid, Grandpa's face was beaming as his weakened legs climbed from branch to branch, finally arriving on the smooth pine floor of E-Wally's new home.

Later that afternoon the sun streamed through the two-foot square open window directly across from the tree house doorway. Leaping from the window ledge to the floor and back to the window, Xena merrily gobbled up small insects and bugs that blew in with the light breeze. A pool of sunny warmth spread across the green flowered scrap of carpet in the center of the smooth wood floor where E-Wally and Grandpa sat cross-legged. "E-Wally," Grandpa began, suddenly a bit more serious as he leaned against the tree house wall, getting more comfortable. "Tell me why you came here?"

E-Wally, wondering if he was finally about to be punished for running away, blurted in a rush, "I had to find a way to save you...and...King Henry is killing you! I couldn't stay and watch it happen. I ran away without a plan. I just wanted to get away. When I first got here I was really scared half crazy and I thought

I'd done something incredibly wrong, really bad. Is that what you think?"

"I don't think you were wrong. You were very brave. It took a hero's bravery to pass through the server and battle the spiders. Plan or no plan, it took some courage to venture here to a strange hard drive. Many e-boys would have stopped, no matter how much they loved their family, but you went all the way past the server."

"Something just made me bolt from the rules, the work, and King Henry's stupid commands. It was super scary being in the hard drive at first. But now I love it here — free of Olla and Henry. I just wish Mom, Maxter, Eddie, and Pete could be here too."

Before Grandpa had a chance to reply, someone came and tapped on the keyboard. The screen lit up and there were Ruthie and Justin happily peering into the file. "I can't believe you are finally back," shouted Justin.

"I'm back and I'm not alone!"

"You must be the humans that created the plan that saved my grandson from the spider. I saw the spider pinning him down and thought I'd lost him forever."

E-Wally interrupted. Turning his back toward Justin and Ruthie, he pulled his shirt out and said, "See, look at the way the mutant's razor-sharp feet shredded my shirt right through my uniform." Then E-Wally told the incredible tale to his friends.

After Justin and Ruthie went to seven grocery dot.com websites to gather a feast of clipart food, and made a stop to download a wild surfer outfit for Grandpa, things settled down. Cuddled close to the screen on Justin's desk, Ruthie and Justin felt like they were right there when Grandpa began to spin one of his wonderful tales they had heard so much about. But this time it was no ordinary tale, as E-Liam was ready to share the story of his younger days, back in the beginning of the Internet.

The children traveled back to the 1970s with E-Liam, and they were mesmerized by the story of those times all the way up to the present day. After some time he paused to inquire if the children wanted to hear more. "Grandpa, sure, finish it if you're not too tired."

E-Liam was neither tired nor thirsty from all of his storytelling, so he continued. "Henry and Olla took over the Council of the Minds and replaced it with the Control of Information. They got into partnership with the profit-mongering, self-serving businessmen. It was right after that that my son Anzwar left to organize the Renegades."

One by one the kids fell sound asleep. They each dreamed epic adventures about Cyberlina, the Stealth Carriers, and mysterious Uncle Anzwar.

The morning light didn't exactly rise slowly on the horizon for E-Wally and Grandpa. In the tree house file saved in Justin's hard drive, morning arrived in a flash. Light burst into the monitor at the unholy hour of 5 A.M. because inquisitive Ruthie couldn't sleep a moment longer. There was a click and then a crackling as the monitor flashed on. E-Wally and Grandpa squinted their eyes in the bright light.

Ruthie had become a regular in Justin's bedroom and this was highly out of the ordinary. Usually Ruthie was sent off with a "get out of my room!" if she ever dared appear uninvited into Justin's private space. Now the siblings were engrossed in a powerful mystery. What was E-Wally's destiny? Would he have to leave? Where would E-Wally need to go to find Anzwar? What else would Grandpa reveal about the mysterious Land of the Internet that buzzed inches, no miles...well, a world away, just outside their own world.

"Hey, want some company?" Ruthie typed, sticking her favorite floppy disk into Justin's hard drive and opening her file.

With a quick cut and paste a bounding Xena scrambled up the tree house rope, leaped, and landed right on Grandpa's stomach. "Oooooof!" went Grandpa.

It was time for Grandpa to wake up and finish telling E-Wally everything. Ruthie had to know more and she wanted to know it right now. "Why did you call your son Anzwar a renegade? Is he bad? My computer thesaurus told me that a renegade was a traitor. That's bad, isn't it?"

E-Wally, listening from the warm coziness of his sleeping bag, had only one memory of Uncle Anzwar; it played like a dim video in E-Wally's mind. He remembered a rust colored beard on a tan face, an easy smile, and a great curly ponytail to grab on. E-Wally also remembered strong, muscular arms reaching into his crib then funny, spinning "hyper flying" as Uncle Anzwar would soar baby E-Wally around. The sounds of Anzwar's deep barrel laugh and his own baby giggles replayed for E-Wally. "What do you mean? Anzwar is not a traitor, he's not bad. He went to find a way to save the e-people. Tell her Grandpa."

Ruthie was not ready to stop asking her own questions in order to listen just yet. "I found so many sites about renegades, outposts, and even pirates. There was one site all about a role-playing game called the Outpost Renegades. Lots of people had huge worlds invented on it. Is that where Anzwar is?" But Ruthie didn't wait for Grandpa to answer. She shot out dozens more questions. Ruthie's fast and furious typing woke sleepy-headed Justin. He stumbled from his bed over to his computer to sit next to his sister.

E-Wally snapped out of his own private thoughts. "Grandpa, tell me where Anzwar is. I just know he's not a traitor. You know everything. You must know what he is doing. I am right, aren't I?" E-Wally pleaded with his grandfather to tell him what he so desperately wanted to know.

"Yes, E-Wally," was the answer E-Wally wanted to hear. That was not the answer he got. Instead, E-Liam replied, "I don't know E-Wally. I'm sorry that I can't tell you what you want to know — where your uncle is or what he's doing." E-Liam's usually sparkling eyes glossed over with a look of pain. "You're partially right in your memory of Anzwar. Your Uncle Anzwar, my own son, was twenty years old when he left. You were just a baby. That was the day he gathered his first small band of renegades and they took off for a place they'd heard of. It was called The OutPost. They got out of the Stealth Carrier zones immediately. They had to escape before the Control got even stronger and they would be trapped like we are. We have been waiting ten years for them to return with a plan to save us, to set things right, to find a way to unhypnotize Algor, and bring back the Council of the Minds."

"Did you think that he was the hero?" Justin asked.

"No," said E-Liam though it was tough to be so honest. "I loved Anzwar as much as any father has ever loved his son, but by the time he was twenty, Anzwar's heart was full of hate. When he began to speak of destroying Henry's reign, I knew somewhere deep inside me that a man with a heart full of anger could not be our long awaited great hero. E-Wally, I know that you have many great and dangerous adventures ahead of you, perhaps through them you will find Anzwar. You're as brave as he ever was and I've never seen a stronger hyper transport rider. Don't forget, you're different from your uncle. Your actions are fueled by love — love for me, love for your mother and Maxter, and love for your people. You don't speak of destroying Henry but of saving your own people. There is a big difference, a big big difference."

Grandpa reached out for E-Wally's hand, pulling him out of the sleeping bag and to his feet. Justin and Ruthie gave each other a questioning look, then focused back on Grandpa who said, "That is why I want you to have this."

With that, Grandpa reached for the chain that was hanging around his neck. E-Wally had never noticed it before. The chain was made of a satin-finished black metal link. It was long — the pendant hung halfway down Grandpa's chest. Grandpa lifted the pendant from inside his shirt and held it carefully.

"Ooooh," exclaimed Ruthie and Justin together as E-Liam held the necklace out for them to see.

What a strange looking design. The pendent was about the size of a quarter with a spiderweb-like design permeating out from a tiny, brilliant crystal that protruded from the center. "This necklace was a gift from Setag. Setag and I spent many hours before the fall of the Council of the Minds discussing the future of the Internet," Grandpa said, holding the pendant on the palm of his hand. "Setag was my human teacher. In fact, he was almost like a brother to me during those hard years as the Council was breaking apart. He shared many secrets with me. That knowledge kept me going all those years when other e-people my age couldn't handle their workload and were scooped up by Olla Brac's bugs."

The kids said nothing. Their eyes were riveted on the pendant. "Whoever learns how to activate this talisman will be guided on their quest to reinstate the Council of the Minds. Only then will King Henry and all his evil droids, bugs, and allies of the Control of Information be overturned."

"Why didn't you give this to Anzwar when he left?" asked E-Wally, trying to make sense of all of this. "If what Setag said was true, how could Anzwar be expected to save the e-people without it?" he said in defense of his uncle.

"I tried," said Grandpa earnestly, holding the pendant toward E-Wally. "You see, when Setag gave it to me he said, 'This is for the answer.' At the time I heard the word 'answer' and thought he meant that the talisman was for Anzwar, but that was not so. When it came time to say good-bye to Anzwar I tried to remove the pendant from my neck, but it wouldn't come off. I was confused. I wondered what sort of charm Setag had hung about my neck. That was when I knew for sure that Anzwar would never be our leader."

The children had not breathed a word since Grandpa began the amazing story. "Just last night I felt the pendant lighten. It lifted a bit as though a rush of air had raised it off my neck. I knew it was time to hand the talisman over to you, E-Wally."

E-Wally felt very calm inside and it surprised him. He caught Ruthie's eye and gave her a suddenly shy smile. She smiled back. It felt weird, but right, to be in this situation — a hero? How odd. Grandpa lifted the chain from around his neck and slowly placed it over E-Wally's head. As the chain and the pendant touched his chest there was a warm feeling that raced through E-Wally like electricity. A zap-crackling of brilliant blue bolts danced from E-Wally's chest and around his entire body.

Justin, Ruthie, and Grandpa gasped a collective, "Whoooooaaaaaah."

Out on the backbone of the Internet, a powerful blue current surged through all the routes, zapping the hair of each fuzzball router straight out and high over their heads. Each quickly grabbed at their wild hair and immediately covered up their funky bodies again. It all happened in a flash. No e-people had seen the routers' chests, which were covered with five stripes of unique and individual colors of their home country. King Henry had decreed years earlier that the routers must grow their hair long to cover them from head to knees so they would all be identical. King

Henry had convinced the routers that they had something that was better than personal colors and individuality – group control over the e-people.

One lone fuzzball router, far away in the nether regions of the Land of the Internet, gathered up all his hair from his head to his toes and tied it high above his head. The vibrant crimson, blue, and green stripes that covered his body blazed boldly. G. Norts was tired of all this – tired of control. He missed the days of thinking, being a guide, and being part of the huge democracy of information that was the Land of the Internet. As the powerful surge brushed past him, he knew in his heart that the rumors he had heard were true. The hero had been found. G. Norts knew it was time for change.

When the surge hit the Royal Castle, it slammed the Control Room doors shut with a bang, but no one noticed. Olla sat smushed into a chair three sizes too small for her bulk, trying to be as inconspicuous as possible. Henry stormed around the room, pounding on his keyboard and calling up information from his database again and again. It was as if he could not believe what Olla had done. He tried to change the outcome of her ruined search by searching the database repeatedly.

"Mutant spiders. You're so proud of your horrible and mutated bugs. Where is the mere e-boy? Why isn't he here neatly wrapped in a web? Instead you've spent all day traveling to a decoy website. What use is an enormous text file filled with the e-boy's name? And look at this," he said, waving a printout in front of Olla's grotesquely devastated face.

She wished with all her might that Henry had not printed out that image of E-Wally standing arrogantly with "Come and get me, Olla" printed on his chest. His lips were pulled unnaturally wide across his face and his tongue wagged tauntingly at them.

Henry crushed the paper into a tight wad and pitched it directly at Sebastian who was standing at attention by the throne. The paper wad spun at Sebastian's feet for a moment.

"Three of the Stealth Carrier line are now free, ready to overtake my power at their first opportunity."

In a desperate voice Olla cried, "Dear King, fear not, I will capture them. I ... I ... I have a new plan ... a plan to unleash at first light."

"I hardly think so," stormed Henry, willing to lose the services of his right-hand demolition queen. "I banish you to your swampy cavern. Be gone, you model of uselessness, princess of the creepy-crawling underlife." He spat at Olla and then turned to the small army of e-servants that he had called to his Control Room. "Lock her in," he said coldly. He stormed out of the room as Olla was netted by the multitude of e-servants.

A moment later, Sebastian looked tentatively from

side to side; no one was there in the room. He cautiously picked up the paper and smoothed it out carefully. With enormous pride and longing he looked at the picture. Olla was banished, and E-Liam was free forever. "You did it," he said pressing his son's picture to his chest. "You've discovered your Quest."

ACKNOWLEDGMENTS

Many thanks go to the team that brought our book through production, beginning with Wilson C. Atkinson for his wise advice and counsel. We received incredible guidance from Pneuma Books: Complete Publisher's Services, especially Brian and Nina Taylor. E-Wally came to life through the creative genius of Jonathon Wilson of JW Studios. Special thanks to Peter Schulz who made our fantasy tale speak to reality through his guidance and technical expertise.

✳

The production of a book is never accomplished by authors simply pounding at a keyboard. Real life inspired us and many people enriched us as we lived the situations that fueled our story. Ms. Shasek would be remiss not to thank two most influential middle school mentors: Sean B. who taught her most everything she knows about web authoring and the power of kids teaching each other; and Derek T., for his whirlwind energy and tech-curiosity. Many thanks go to the pioneering imagination of Al Weis, Seymour Papert, Teresa Amabile, Dennis Harper and Annie Dillard. This diverse group of experts flavored her mission, her writing and educational philosophy. Ms. Schulz would like to thank her father who has taught her that the path less traveled holds the greatest rewards. His life example has given her the strength to be the master of her own fate even when others call her plans impossible. A heartfelt thanks goes to Ms. Schulz's mother for her everyday example of all that public education can and should be and her continuing commitment to helping every child find their quest.

✦

01000010 01100101 01110111 01100001 01110010 01100101 00100000
01101111 01100110 00100000 01110100 01101000 01100101 00100000
01000111 01101100 01101111 01100010 01100001 01101100 00100000
01001000 01100001 01100011 01101011 01100101 01110010 00100000
01000111 01100001 01101110 01100111 00101110 00101110 00101110
01000010 01100101 01110111 01100001 01110010 01100101 00100000
01101111 01100110 00100000 01110100 01101000 01100101 00100000
01000111 01101100 01101111 01100010 01100001 01101100 00100000
01001000 01100001 01100011 01101011 01100101 01110010 00100000
01000111 01100001 01101110 01100111 00101110 00101110 00101110
01000010 01100101 01110111 01100001 01110010 01100101 00100000
01101111 01100110 00100000 01110100 01101000 01100101 00100000
01000111 01101100 01101111 01100010 01100001 01101100 00100000
01001000 01100001 01100011 01101011 01100101 01110010 00100000
01000111 01100001 01101110 01100111 00101110 00101110 00101110
01000010 01100101 01110111 01100001 01110010 01100101 00100000
01101111 01100110 00100000 01110100 01101000 01100101 00100000
01000111 01101100 01101111 01100010 01100001 01101100 00100000
01001000 01100001 01100011 01101011 01100101 01110010 00100000
01000111 01100001 01101110 01100111 00101110 00101110 00101110
01000010 01100101 01110111 01100001 01110010 01100101 00100000
01101111 01100110 00100000 01110100 01101000 01100101 00100000
01000111 01101100 01101111 01100010 01100001 01101100 00100000
01001000 01100001 01100011 01101011 01100101 01110010 00100000
01000111 01100001 01101110 01100111 00101110 00101110 00101110
01000010 01100101 01110111 01100001 01110010 01100101 00100000
01101111 01100110 00100000 01110100 01101000 01100101 00100000
01000111 01101100 01101111 01100010 01100001 01101100 00100000
01001000 01100001 01100011 01101011 01100101 01110010 00100000
01000111 01100001 01101110 01100111 00101110 00101110 00101110
01000010 01100101 01110111 01100001 01110010 01100101 00100000
01101111 01100110 00100000 01110100 01101000 01100101 00100000
01000111 01101100 01101111 01100010 01100001 01101100 00100000
01001000 01100001 01100011 01101011 01100101 01110010 00100000
01000111 01100001 01101110 01100111 00101110 00101110 00101110
01000010 01100101 01110111 01100001 01110010 01100101 00100000
01101111 01100110 00100000 01110100 01101000 01100101 00100000